THE PARKER WOMEN

KAY CORRELL

This book is dedicated to my husband. I could not have made it through the last few years without his unwavering support.
You are my hero.

story between series - with Josephine and Paul from The Letter.)

LIGHTHOUSE POINT ~ THE SERIES
Wish Upon a Shell - Book One
Wedding on the Beach - Book Two
Love at the Lighthouse - Book Three
Cottage near the Point - Book Four
Return to the Island - Book Five
Bungalow by the Bay - Book Six

CHARMING INN ~ Return to Lighthouse Point
One Simple Wish - Book One
Two of a Kind - Book Two
Three Little Things - Book Three
Four Short Weeks - Book Four
Five Years or So - Book Five
Six Hours Away - Book Six
Charming Christmas - Book Seven

SWEET RIVER ~ THE SERIES
A Dream to Believe in - Book One
A Memory to Cherish - Book Two
A Song to Remember - Book Three
A Time to Forgive - Book Four
A Summer of Secrets - Book Five

A Moment in the Moonlight - Book Six

MOONBEAM BAY ~ THE SERIES (2021)
The Parker Women - Book One (Jan 2021)
The Parker Cafe - Book Two (Feb 2021)
A Heather Parker Original - Book Three
The Parker Family Secret - Book Four
Grace Parker's Peach Pie - Book Five

INDIGO BAY ~ A multi-author sweet romance series

Sweet Days by the Bay - Kay's Complete Collection of stories in the Indigo Bay series

Or buy them separately:

Sweet Sunrise - Book Three
Sweet Holiday Memories - A short holiday story
Sweet Starlight - Book Nine

Sign up for my newsletter at my website *kaycorrell.com* to make sure you don't miss any new releases or sales.

CHAPTER 1

Donna Foster closed and locked the door to Parker's General Store. She paused and swept her glance down the long brick road in front of the store. Couples leisurely wandered the sidewalk and gathered together, talking and laughing. Luckily for her, Moonbeam was a safe little coastal town sitting right on the edge of Moonbeam Bay. Most nights she walked home after closing up Parker's.

She glanced up at the clear blue sky. Full moon tonight. She couldn't wait to get home, sit out, and watch the stars come out and the moon rise.

She deserved a small break, didn't she? She'd worked ten days straight, which wasn't that unusual. As owner of the store, it wasn't like she could just walk away and let it run itself. But a day off now and then would be nice.

She smiled and touched the small plaque by the door that proclaimed, established in 1926, like she always did as she left. Whether it was a superstition or just her way of thanking her great-grandparents who opened the store all those years ago, she wasn't certain. But a quick touch as she closed the shop had become her routine after she took over running the store.

She turned and headed down Magnolia Avenue, anxious to get home.

"Donna, wait up."

She turned when she heard Evelyn's voice.

Her sister hurried up to her, dressed in what could only be called country-club casual, or cruise-casual, or something much nicer than Donna's own work outfit. But then, Evelyn looked just as put together for an evening out on the town as she did for a brief run to the market.

"Hey, Ev," she greeted her sister.

"Do you want to go get something to eat with me? I was thinking of trying that new place on the wharf, Portside Grill."

"Is Darren still out of town?"

A flicker of uneasiness passed across

Evelyn's features but was quickly hidden with a bright smile.

"He is."

"He's been gone a long time this time, hasn't he?"

"His business keeps him very busy." Evelyn didn't quite answer the question about her husband's whereabouts.

Torn between her desire to go home and relax and the fact her sister obviously wanted some company, she held back a sigh and nodded. "Sure, dinner sounds great."

"Perfect." Evelyn bobbed her head, and her thick hair, carefully curled, bounced around her shoulders without a strand of gray in sight.

Donna knew that if she looked in a mirror right now, there would be clear evidence of gray hair at her temples and her mostly brown hair would be an unruly mess of curls. But then, Evelyn had always been the pretty sister. The popular sister. The one who got the admiring looks, while she got the well-that's-unfortunate sympathy looks when compared to Evelyn.

Not that any of that mattered. It was what it was. And they were friends. Usually. Mostly. Except when they disagreed with their strong opinions that often went in divergent directions.

"Come on, Ev. Let's go. I am starving."
They linked arms, headed down the street, and
turned the corner to walk out onto the long pier
at the wharf, ready to try the newest restaurant
in their small town.

Olivia Foster waved to her cousin, who was
threading her way toward her through the
packed tables of Jimmy's, their favorite
restaurant on the wharf. The wooden high-top
tables with layer upon layer of lacquer polished
by years of use provided guests with the best
view of the bay out over the long railings.

Although there was some inside seating,
hardly anyone ever sat in there except maybe on
especially cold days in winter, which were few
and far between. And still, even then, Olivia
preferred to sit outside. Jimmy's served up fried
food, cold beer, and the best hushpuppies in
Florida, if she was any judge of hushpuppies
—and she was.

Heather smiled and waved back, then
enveloped Olivia in a hug when she got to the
table. "Livy, so great to see you. I've missed
you."

"Sit down. Tell me all about your trip to Portland. I was going to order you a drink but wasn't sure if it was a beer night or wine night for you."

"I'll have a beer."

"Me, too." Olivia caught the server's attention and motioned for two beers. The server was a regular and knew their favorite beer was a local craft beer.

Heather slipped into the seat across from her and let out a long breath. "Ah, I really do love this place. It always feels like I'm really home when I get here."

"I thought about checking out the new restaurant, Portside Grill, that just opened on the wharf, but why mess with a good thing?"

"I'll be here a while. We can check it out some day next week."

"Sounds good to me. But for now? I'm having a fish taco and a side of hushpuppies."

"Of course you are." Heather grinned. "I'm going to have a chef salad."

"Really? So I can feel guilty?" She gave her cousin a stern look.

Heather laughed. "Okay, fish tacos and hushpuppies for me, too."

"Much better." The server came back with

their beers and took their orders. Olivia took a sip of the ice-cold beer. "So good."

Heather took a sip of hers and looked out over the water. "Going to be a brilliant sunset tonight."

"The skies are just showing off for you. Letting you know what you've missed while you were gone."

"Anything big happen while I was away?"

Olivia grinned. "In Moonbeam? I don't think so. Does anything big ever happen here?"

"I heard The Cabot Hotel got bought out by some big-time hotel guy and they're rehabbing it to reopen. I think that's great. It used to be such a grand place. It had that wide porch wrapping around it with rockers looking over the bay. It's a shame it was left to ruin." Heather leaned back and grinned. "Remember when we used to sneak over and get ice cream there? Always felt guilty because we weren't getting it at Parker's."

"I do remember that." Olivia nodded. "I think I heard it's been closed for over ten years. Can't believe it's been that long. I'm sure there's a ton of work to get it up to code and back open."

"Well, I'm glad it's happening."

"So what's new with you?" Contrary to Olivia's own life, her cousin always seemed to have something new and exciting going on.

"I got a new contract with a card company for my illustrations. This series is kind of beachy themed." Despite Heather's modest expression, Olivia knew Heather was proud of her accomplishments. "If that works out, the company will expand to some other items and put my illustrations on coasters, tote bags, wall signs. Things like that. And I have another company interested in all those coffee illustrations."

"That's fantastic. I love your work. That last series you did on friendship with all those women of different ages and the different friendships? That was great."

"I do like to doodle." Heather shrugged.

Olivia burst out laughing. She loved this cousin of hers, her best friend. As close as someone could get to being a sister without actually being one. "*Doodles?* That's what you call your artwork?"

Their conversation was cut short by the delivery of their meals, and Heather deftly changed the subject to her travels while Olivia listened to the tales of adventure. Heather loved to travel, and she claimed she could get her inspiration for her art anywhere. The travel lust had started when Heather was barely old enough to escape Moonbeam and her constant conflicts with her father. Heather had left home right after high school—which was great for Heather, but it had left an empty spot in Olivia's life.

"So, how's that daughter of yours, my favorite almost-daughter?" Heather changed the subject from her travels.

"Emily's doing great. Of course. I mean... I'm not sure what I did to deserve a kid like her. She's helping mom and me at Parker's, and she's taken another job at the history museum."

"She's a hard worker."

"She saves most of it for college. Although, she's also hoping to get some scholarship money."

"Wouldn't be surprised if she does. Isn't she like first in her class?"

Olivia beamed with pride. "She is. But she works really hard for it."

"I'm proud of her, too. Can't wait to see her."

"She's working at Parker's tomorrow. You should stop in."

"I think I will." Heather yawned. "But for now, I'm sorry. I'm beat. I just dropped my suitcase at my apartment and rushed over here. I should go unpack, throw some laundry in the washer, and check my mail. Get back to real life."

Olivia stood. "Sure. We'll meet up again later this week."

"Sounds good to me."

They headed out of Jimmy's and strolled down the long pier lined with shops on each side. White twinkle lights strung along the shop fronts made the whole walkway look magical. A lone singer sat with his guitar, singing a ballad at one of the outside cafes.

Olivia looked down the long pier and laughed. "Look who's here. Like mothers, like daughters, I guess."

Heather glanced down the pier. "Ah..." A rueful look crossed her face. "This won't go well..."

Olivia waved and caught their attention. Her mother and Aunt Evelyn walked up to them, and a careful, neutral expression settled on Heather's face as she hugged her mother. Family dynamics were always difficult in her cousin's family...

"I didn't know you were back in town, Heather." Aunt Evelyn frowned, an accusing tone in her voice. "Donna, did you know she was back? You didn't tell me."

"Just got here, Mom. Like minutes ago," Heather assured her.

"What are you two doing here?" Olivia asked as she hugged her mom.

"We went to the new restaurant," her mother said.

"How was it?"

"It was really nice. We enjoyed it." Aunt Evelyn's eyes still held a bit of a reproachful look for Heather. "I supposed you two were at Jimmy's?"

"But of course." Olivia nodded. "Got to welcome Heather back home in style." Maybe if she just prattled a bit, Aunt Evelyn would quit frowning.

"Do you two want to get a drink with us? We were going to sit out here and listen to the music and enjoy a glass of wine." Her mother offered up an invitation, either oblivious to the undercurrent between Heather and Aunt Evelyn, or, more likely, ignoring it.

"I'm pretty beat." Heather shook her head.

"I've had a long day, too." Olivia chimed in. "I think I'm just going to head home."

"Okay, well, we should all get together while Heather's back in town," her mother insisted. "I'll set something up."

"That would be great," Heather said unconvincingly. "Come on, Livy, I'll walk part way home with you."

They turned and strolled the rest of the way down the pier. Olivia wanted to broach the subject of Heather and her mother, but really, what was there to say? They'd never been that close. Aunt Evelyn was kind of a walled-off, self-protecting person. Her aunt had been that way for almost as long as she could remember.

She'd been the lucky cousin with her own mother, and she thanked her lucky stars every day.

"We could sneak a drink out on the lanai at my house." Olivia tapped Heather's arm. "They'd never find out. Or are you too tired?"

"You know, I'd like that. I love your view. You're lucky to live on the waterway system." A small smile lit Heather's face. "And real life is over-rated. It can wait."

"I am lucky. I love that it faces the sunsets and that Emily and I both have our own rooms.

It is nice. But you have a view of the bay from your balcony."

"Somehow a one-bedroom condo in a four-floor complex doesn't really feel like a home like your place does." Heather shrugged. "But it works for the small amount of time I'm in town. I just need someplace to call mine and have my mail sent to."

They entered her home, and she grabbed a bottle of Pinot Grigio from the fridge. They headed to a pair of Adirondack chairs out on the lanai. The whole patio area was screened in —she was forever grateful for its defense against mosquitos and no-see-ums that plagued the area during the spring and summer months, especially when heavy rains and high tides would stir up the mosquitos in the mangroves lining much of the waterways.

She lived where two waterways converged, and one flowed on out to the harbor. Many of her neighbors had huge boats sitting at docks by their homes. She and Emily had an old fifteen-foot fishing boat that she constantly had to encourage to run. But she did like puttering around the canals. They often took it over to her mother's house nearby, too. It was closer by water than driving, like so much in Moonbeam's twisted canal system.

They settled into the chairs and Heather kicked off her shoes. "So, do you know if my dad is in town or not?"

"I haven't seen him for months. Not that he comes into Parker's much anyway. Mom hasn't said anything about him."

Heather sighed. "I'm hoping he's out of town the whole time I'm here."

"How long do you plan on staying this time?" Olivia crossed her fingers that her cousin was planning a nice, long visit.

"I'm not sure. A month or so, maybe."

Olivia would take that. It was longer than she usually got with her. She raised her glass. "To a nice long visit."

Heather nodded, touched glasses, and they both took a sip of the delicious wine. And somehow, things seemed right in the world, sitting here with Heather just like they'd done so many nights before.

CHAPTER 2

B arry Richmond strode into the lobby of The Cabot Hotel. His friend Delbert Hamilton had made him an offer he couldn't refuse. Come finish up coordinating the remodel and opening of the hotel. The offer held a very tempting salary plus a bonus if everything was finished on time. But he'd wanted to come see the old hotel before he gave Delbert his final answer.

From his research, he knew the place had sat empty for many years. That is, until Delbert decided to buy it and add it into his eclectic chain of Hamilton Hotels. Del had been working on getting it reopened but had a series of mishaps. He needed someone here to manage everything. The rehab, the hiring, the re-opening. All of which were right up Barry's alley. He was often hired to open either new hotels or hotels that had been rehabbed. He'd stay for a year or so, then move onto the next job. Didn't make for a steady personal life, but he enjoyed the work.

Delbert came bustling up to him and reached out a hand. "There you are. Glad you made it."

He returned Del's firm handshake. "Wanted to take a look before giving you my answer."

"I'm hoping to convince you that your answer is yes, you'll take on the job. I've been trying to coordinate it, but between the other Hamilton Hotels and the fairly new one we've opened in Sarasota, I'm spreading myself too thin. The man who usually helps with this, Adam Lyons, is working on The Beverly, a new hotel that I'm opening in Tampa. But I need a strong leader in here at The Cabot who can jump in and make this happen."

There was scaffolding scattered through the lobby, and on his way in, he'd noticed the steps to the wide front porch had yet to be repaired and repainted.

"I know, it looks like not a lot has been done, but it has. The kitchen has been updated. Most of the upstairs rooms are updated. Plumbing was redone. Still having some problems with electric. But there's still so much. Plus hiring. I've been unable to find a good full-time manager, though I do have some staff hired. But we'll need other staff, especially that manager."

"When are you planning on opening?"

"We're planning on opening in a few more months, three at most, but I don't want to pick a firm date until I'm sure we'll make it."

"So, what made you choose this place?"

"Because..." Delbert raised a hand and swung his arm wide. "She's a grand old lady, isn't she? Just needs a bit of love. I want to restore her to how magnificent she used to be. She has so much history."

"She's got beautiful bones. Did the last owners just not put the cash back into her to keep her updated?"

"No, they didn't. Cashflow problems, I heard. Which was why, after a storm came through and did some damage, they didn't reopen it. The town was actually in talks to try and get it torn down, but its historical value protected it for a bit."

"Lucky for you. And that's where you came in."

"Precisely." Delbert led him through the lobby and out onto the wide plank porch that stretched the length of the hotel. Repairs were being made to the tall pillars supporting the upper balconies above them.

"Wow, this view. It's spectacular." He turned to Del. "Okay, you've convinced me. I'll take it. I'd love to see this hotel returned to her former glory. She's from a bygone era of hotels. Let's see if we can bring her back."

Delbert grinned and clasped his hand, pumping it quickly. "Great. Great news. When can you start?"

"Today?" He smiled at his friend as he began to roll up his shirt sleeves. "And tomorrow I'll wear something that's a bit more appropriate for your weather down here."

"Perfect. I was hoping you'd say yes. I've already spoken with a realtor. Found you a rental on the waterways. It's nice, quiet, and you'll have a dock if you're a fisherman. It's included in my offer to you."

A place to live already procured. That was one thing off his list. He'd half-expected he'd just stay in a hotel somewhere nearby. But the privacy and peace of a house sounded nice.

"Haven't fished in years, but I could probably be talked into it if I have time."

"Here, I'll show you the room I've taken over for an office. It's all yours now. And let me show you the rest of the hotel."

He took one last look at the bay. A large sailboat sliced across the water in the distance. On the far side of the bay, he could barely see land. He took in a deep breath of the salty air. He was going to enjoy this job. So much nicer than his last job in the noise and pollution of the city.

He turned and followed Delbert inside, eager to get to work.

Donna finished up her early morning chores. She had just enough time to throw in some laundry and pick up a bit. The house was way more space than she needed, but she loved it. It had been her grandparents' house, and she and Evelyn had spent so much time here when they were growing up.

After she'd inherited the house, she had wonderful memories of when Olivia and Emily had lived here with her, too. They'd stayed until

Emily was about eight, but then Olivia had insisted they needed a place of their own. Luckily, they'd found the small house nearby and Donna had helped with the down payment.

Olivia loved having her own place with Emily, and Donna had—eventually—adjusted to living here alone. Her instincts had wanted her to beg them to stay, not leave her. But she knew that was her own insecurities speaking and that she had to let her daughter spread her wings a bit. And it wasn't like Olivia actually *left* her—she told herself that often and loudly —Olivia had just grown up and wanted her independence and a place to raise Emily on her own.

But she was grateful that she'd been able to help her daughter when she got pregnant with Emily at only nineteen. She'd been there for her every step of the way. Not that she'd learned how to be a good mother from her own mom, but that was something Donna had made peace with. Kinda of. Pretty much so.

She glanced at the calendar on the wall. Speaking of her mother, she should be in some European city today. Who knew which one? There was a full itinerary printed out here somewhere of the world tour her mother was taking with a handful of people from her fancy retirement village. She'd gotten one photo and text with her mother in front of the Eiffel Tower in Paris, and one photo—no words with it—of her mom on a cute wooden bridge somewhere in Switzerland. She wasn't even sure when her mother planned on returning. Not that it mattered much. They rarely saw each other. Her mom had even made an excuse for why she couldn't come to Moonbeam for Christmas this last year. She wondered if Evelyn had heard from her recently. She hadn't even thought to ask her sister the other night at dinner at Portside Grill.

She took one last look around, knowing the place really needed a deep clean, but who had the time? Ignoring the nagging thought, she headed outside. A lone man was leaving the rental house next door. The Meyers must have found a new renter. They only did longer-term rentals, and she was grateful for that. It helped prevent loud, weekend partier rentals. She locked the door and turned, intending on greeting her new temporary neighbor. She lifted a hand in a wave, but the man didn't see her, engrossed in his own thoughts, and hurried off with brisk strides.

At a more leisurely pace, she followed him down the street, enjoying the sunshine. She loved the early mornings when not many were up and about. Never really minded being out before many in the town were stirring and being the person to open the store. Though it looked like her new neighbor was an early riser, too.

She got to the store, unlocked it, and flipped the sign to open. So began her day, just like the day before, and the day before that.

Olivia hurried into Parker's mid-morning. She waved to her mom, who was busy with a customer, and went over to the small area at the side of the store where they had a long counter and a few small tables. Parker's had always had a small malt shop area in the store. At first, it had been her great-grandmother's homemade ice cream, one flavor a day, that townspeople flocked to come and enjoy in cones. Her great-grandmother had taken over running the store from her own parents and added the ice cream shop as her own special flair in the general store. Eventually, the tiny corner for ice cream expanded, so they had a handful of flavors, started making malts, and added a soda fountain.

This part of the store wasn't very profitable anymore, and to make it profitable, they really needed more space to expand to a larger selection of food items. But there really was no more space to expand into without giving up something else in the store. Her mother made noises about changing it, but neither one of them could quite give up the history of the malt shop. And it did bring in people to the store, who then often remembered something else they needed to pick up.

She put on an apron and scooted behind the counter. The malt shop counter opened up about eleven a.m. each day until they closed the store in the evening. She looked up as her first customer approached. "Mr. Hamilton, hi. What's your pleasure?"

"Butter pecan. Two scoops today. I'm calling it my late breakfast." He winked at her.

"I think ice cream should always qualify as a meal." She grinned back. He'd become a regular customer here since he bought The Cabot Hotel. Sometimes just a fountain soda —always with extra ice—and sometimes a cone or a malt.

She carefully dished him up a waffle cone with his ice cream and handed it to him. He slipped onto a stool to eat it as he often did, staying and chatting with her. She got a malt for another customer and turned back to Mr. Hamilton. "Things going okay with the work on the hotel?"

"They are now. Hired someone else to manage the day-to-day. Barry Richmond. Met him years ago and thankfully he was available for the job now. I need to go check on a hotel we're opening in Tampa, and there's a problem at one of our older hotels in Philadelphia. Going to be gone for a bit."

"We'll miss you."

He smiled. "And I'll miss your ice cream."

"We'll be here when you get back."

"You'll be one of my first stops when I do return."

"Hi, Mom," Emily called out as she breezed in the door and headed back to the stockroom. Emily always breezed through everywhere, a whirlwind of energy and ambition.

"My daughter, Em. She works here, too." Olivia nodded toward the direction Emily had disappeared. She was pleased to see that Mr. Hamilton's face didn't immediately have the look she usually got when people realized she had a sixteen-year-old daughter.

"She looks like you. Except for the hair."

"I know. Not sure where she got that all that red hair. She's forever fighting to tame it, but it kind of has a mind of its own." Why was she explaining her daughter's hair to Mr. Hamilton? Although he was an easy one to talk to, she doubted a teen's hair problems were big on his chatting list.

"I used to know a girl with hair like that." He smiled and stood. "I should go. But one other thing I'd like."

"What's that?"

"Call me, Del, please. Mr. Hamilton... I keep thinking you're speaking to my father." His eyes twinkled with friendliness.

She grinned. "Del, it is, then. And I'm Olivia—Livy."

"Thanks, Livy. See you when I get back in town."

She watched as he left the store, then turned back to work. She had more vanilla ice cream to make, and things usually picked up here in the afternoon. Better get moving before things got too busy. She sure didn't want to run out of their signature flavor.

CHAPTER 3

Barry headed over to Parker's General Store that evening. Ever since Del dropped by before he left town and mentioned the ice cream there, Barry had been craving a malt. He asked directions from a worker at the hotel who said to head to Magnolia Avenue and he couldn't miss it. He took Harborside, cut across Third Street, and ended up on Magnolia Avenue. The worker was right, you couldn't miss the large sign over the general store. Parker's.

The whole idea of an old-fashioned general store intrigued him. Not to mention one with a malt shop inside. He headed down the block and pushed into the store. Del had said the malt shop was run by a young, friendly woman, Livy.

The woman behind the counter did look friendly, but she appeared to be about his age— and he'd quit thinking of himself as young quite a few years back. He slid onto a stool at the counter.

The woman turned from chatting with a customer and walked over to greet him. "What can I get for you?"

"Are you the Livy who my friend Del raves about? Says she has the best ice cream in the state."

Her mouth swept up into a smile. "Ah, that would be my daughter. But we do have the best ice cream around. My grandmother's recipe."

"Really? So what do you suggest?"

"I always suggest the vanilla malt. My favorite. Our homemade vanilla is delicious." She smiled again. "All the flavors are delicious, if I do say so myself. My grandmother was a genius with recipes of all types."

"Then a vanilla malt it is."

The woman deftly made the malt, said a word or two to the customer at the end of the counter, and greeted two new people who came in and wandered back further into the store. She did all this without missing a beat, then placed the malt in front of him with a straw and a long-handled spoon. "Enjoy."

He took a bite—too large of a bite by the instant cold headache that stabbed his forehead—and acknowledged that everyone was right. Delbert and this woman. It was delicious.

A young teen walked up. "Grams, there are two more customers to check out. I'll get them. Do you need anything else?"

Grams? Though there was a hint of gray threaded through her dark brown hair, he wouldn't have pegged her as a grandmother of a teenager. Though, to be honest, he didn't quite always do the math and it shocked him when he ran into old friends who were grandparents. He certainly wasn't old enough for that. But really, what did he know? He had no kids, so he'd never have a grandkid. Confirmed bachelor. Not that it bothered him. He'd long since made peace with his choices.

The woman's warm voice interrupted his thoughts. "Just check out the Jacksons, then you can head on home. I'll lock up."

"Okay, I'll be in about ten tomorrow and unpack that paint shipment we have coming in."

"Thanks, Em."

The other customer finished his ice cream

and left. He figured he should finish his and let this woman close up. She scrubbed the counter, and as she got nearer to him, she smiled. "No hurry." She tidied up the area and turned back to him, leaning against the counter without a trace of hurrying him along. "So, you in town for vacation?"

"I'm here for quite a while, actually. Working on The Cabot Hotel renovations."

"Really?" Her eyes lit up. "I'm so glad that Mr. Hamilton bought it and is fixing it up. She used to be the most elegant, grand hotel. Back in the 1920s people would come and winter at the hotel. It has a fascinating history. My granddaughter, Emily, works at the history museum and loves all the old stories about the hotel and the town." She reached out her hand. "I'm Donna, by the way."

"Let me guess. Donna Parker."

She grinned. "No, Donna Foster. But the first Parkers to own the shop were my great-grandparents. Parkers are known for having daughters." She shrugged. "So the store got passed down from daughter to daughter, even after the Parker surname died out for our family. But most of the town still refer to us as the Parker women."

"So you inherited it with this generation?"

"I did. My older sister, Evelyn, doesn't have any interest in the store. She's... well, she's busy with other things."

"I see." He nodded toward the young, red-headed girl rushing out of the store with a brief "Bye, Grams."

"And that's your granddaughter?"

"Livy's daughter."

"Ah, the one Delbert attributes the deliciousness of the ice cream to."

"The very one."

"Oh, and I'm Barry. Barry Richmond."

"Nice to meet you, Barry."

He finished the malt and she took the glass from him as he rose. "Thank you. I'm sure I'll be back soon for another one."

"Any time."

He headed out onto Magnolia Avenue and wandered down the street in the direction of his rental.

Or so he thought.

He finally realized he must be turned around and pulled out his phone to look at the map. He'd been walking in the exact wrong direction. With a tired sigh, he turned around and headed back down the street the way he'd come, looking for a Grand Canal Street that should lead him to Sandpiper Court and his rental.

As he passed Parker's, Donna was just closing the front door. She touched a small sign by the door as she turned to leave. He startled her slightly as he approached. "Hello again."

"Oh, Barry. Hi."

"It appears I got a bit turned around when I headed home." He grinned sheepishly. "I think I've got it now though."

"Where are you headed?"

"Sandpiper Court."

She looked at him closely. "On the waterway? Right near the point?"

"I am."

"Ah, you've rented the Meyer's place." She grinned. "Hi, neighbor. I live in the house next door. The two-story on the point."

"That house is wonderful. Love the architecture."

"Been in my family for generations. Since they first built the canal system here to expand the town of Moonbeam. So, you want to walk home together?" She tossed him a grin. "At least you won't get lost again. I'm pretty sure I know the way."

He laughed, suddenly glad to have the company even though he was usually a loner. "It's probably a good idea for me to have a guide."

She cocked her head to one side. "Okay, we go this way."

He fell into step beside her.

Barry and Donna walked down the sidewalk as the warm evening air wrapped around them. Fluffy white thunderheads towered in the sky as the sun began its descent. Donna must have said hi to at least a dozen people as they passed by. She leaned close with remarks such as "he's the CEO at the bank" or "she owns Barbara's Boutique—but her name is Margaret."

They turned off of Magnolia and onto Grand Canal. "See that tree there? That's a poinciana. One of my favorite trees. So pretty in the spring with its limbs full of flowers." She walked at a leisurely pace, and he slowed his normal brisk pace to keep in step, realizing he was in no hurry for their walk to end.

They turned onto Sandpiper Court and she paused in front of his rental.

"Thanks for the tour and all the local information." He paused at the end of the drive.

"Any time." She looked like she was going to say something, but stopped just short. "Well, good night."

"Night."

She crossed the distance and entered into the old house at the end of the cul-de-sac. A light came on inside and spilled a warm glow out onto her front porch.

He turned and headed inside his rental, switching on the light as he entered, trying to make the house seem a bit more homey. Not that he needed homey since most of his life was in corporate apartments or hotel rooms, the absolute definition of *not* homey. But something about Donna's friendly spill-over of warm, yellow light had tugged at something inside of him. Some distant memory of walking through the door at night and that feeling of "ah, I'm home." He hadn't felt that for more years than he could count.

CHAPTER 4

Olivia met Heather at Brewster's on the wharf for coffee the next morning. She grabbed two black coffees and a table overlooking the bay. Heather slipped into the seat beside her moments later. "Cuz."

She slid the coffee cup over to Heather. "Here you go."

"Thanks." Heather dropped her purse onto a chair beside them. "I have missed Brewster's coffee."

"You miss everything when you're gone," Olivia teased. "Jimmy's, Brewster's—oh, and me."

Heather laughed. "So true. I do miss lots about Moonbeam when I'm gone."

"You shouldn't stay away so much. Want to

go out to Pelican Cay this weekend? Em and I are going with Mom and hitting the beach. Haven't been to the beach in a long time."

"That sounds great. I need a beach walk."

Olivia smiled. "I know what you mean. Have to have my beach fix every once in a while. We're taking Mom's boat. Meet us at nine a.m. at her house?"

Heather tilted her head. "This isn't one of Aunt Donna's plans to get Mom and I out together, is it?"

"As far as I know, Aunt Evelyn isn't going. She's not much of a boater anyway, is she?"

"No, not much. They have that long dock wrapping around their property on the bay, but no boat in the slip. Father always said he doesn't have time for boats."

"Though, he does rent out that huge yacht at the marina for his business partners and takes them down to the Keys, doesn't he?"

"He does." Heather shrugged. "Complete with its captain and crew. It's part of his big-shot persona."

There was no warmth in Heather's voice when she talked about her father. "Have you seen your Mom since you've gotten back? Aside from when we ran into her at the wharf, I mean."

"No." Heather let out a long sigh. "I suppose I should stop by. Maybe have tea or something. I don't think Father is home."

She couldn't imagine feeling like it was an unwanted obligation to visit her own mother. She'd often wished that Heather and Aunt Evelyn could work out a better relationship. But it seemed like that wasn't ever going to happen. She missed the days when they were young girls and their moms would take them on outings together. Sometimes they went to the beach. Sometimes into the city for the theatre. But as Heather's father had risen in the ranks of his company, Aunt Evelyn had spent more time throwing business parties and running very visible charity events. And somewhere along the way, Heather and her mother had grown apart.

"Oh, look, there's The Destiny coming back in from her sunrise cruise." Heather pointed to a large, double-decker boat passing by the wharf on its way to the marina.

"I'm glad to see she's still running." Heather looked out over the water.

"I heard that Jesse bought it."

"Really?" Heather's eyebrows rose. "Our Jesse?"

A smile tugged at her mouth. "Yes, *your* Jesse." Heather and Jesse had grown up as next-door neighbors. Well, at least until she'd moved into the huge mansion her parents bought on the bay when Heather was about twelve.

"Well, good for him." Heather watched as the boat slipped passed them.

"Want to stop by the marina after coffee and say hi?"

"What? No... No, I have things I need to do."

"If you say so. I bet he'd like to see you."

"Don't be silly."

"I'm not being silly. You two were great friends."

"That was so long ago." Heather shook her head. "Anyway, tell me about the store. Business good?"

"Same as always. Not great, not bad."

"At least you have your job there. It's secure. You do like working there, don't you?"

"I love working there, I do. And it gave me so much flexibility when Emily was young. But sometimes..." She turned and looked out over the bay at the sunlight dancing across the rolling water.

"Sometimes, what?" Heather leaned forward, frowning.

She turned back to her cousin. "Sometimes I wish... I wish I could do more than just work in Mom's store. Do something on my own. Make something of myself that isn't all tied to Parker's. My mom and her grandparents and her great-grandparents are what made Parker's what it is today."

"But you're lucky. You work with your mother and you two get along. You help her keep the store running smoothly. You did all this while raising a great daughter."

Olivia laughed. "You make me sound ungrateful, and I'm not. I'm very, very lucky. I just wonder sometimes... If things had been different..."

"You mean if you wouldn't have had Emily so young?"

Olivia shook her head. "No, not that part. I wouldn't change a thing about that. Emily is my everything." She let out a sigh. "I just wonder what I could have done with my life. Accomplished. If I hadn't just jumped into working in the store."

"There's so much history in that store. I'm sometimes jealous of you working there. I loved that your mother let us play there in the store when we were girls and help out. I'm pretty sure we were more work than help."

A smile teased her lips. "I'm sure we were."

"But you know, you could do anything you wanted now. Emily is older. You're still young." Heather pinned her with a look. "So... what do you want to do?"

"Well... I... I've been taking online classes."

"Why didn't you tell me?"

"I don't know. I didn't know if I'd do very well in them. And it's been a long time since I dropped out of college when I got pregnant with Emily."

"But you're doing well?"

She gave her cousin a sheepish grin. "I'm kind of acing it. Now that I'm studying something I want to learn, I'm finding I'm pretty good at it."

Heather laughed. "I'm not surprised. What are you studying?"

"Business. A smattering of marketing, accounting, and general business."

"Good for you, Liv."

"I finished up my associate's degree that I

started all those years ago, and I'm going to continue until I get my full bachelor's degree."

Heather leaned back, her eyes wide. "Bravo. Of course, you can do that. I'm so proud of you."

She shrugged. "But... what am I going to use it for? I could never leave Parker's. Never leave Mom to run it by herself. Not after all she's done for Em and me."

"Aunt Donna would want you to do whatever you want. Be whatever you want."

"Maybe. But I still couldn't leave Parker's. I'm just hoping some of my knowledge can eventually be used to help run the store. At least I can use it for that."

Heather reached out and covered her hand. "Or, you could fly, my Liv. You could fly. You could do or be anything you want."

CHAPTER 5

Heather said goodbye to Livy and watched her hurry off to work at Parker's. She frowned as she watched her disappear. All that studying. All that education. And why couldn't she leave Parker's? Her cousin deserved to get out on her own if that's what she wanted. Or at least do something to make her mark.

Though, knowing Liv, she'd never leave Parker's. She'd be too afraid of disappointing her mother, of letting her down. And in all honesty, Aunt Donna had been there for Liv and Emily every step of the way. Always supported them even when Liv and Brett decided not to get married when Liv got pregnant. They'd realized they weren't a good fit. And they weren't. Heather was glad Livy hadn't ended up with Brett. She'd never been a fan of his. But Brett popped into town every so often, and Liv said he called Emily fairly regularly.

But... she still wished Liv could have a chance to follow her dreams. *Everyone* should have a chance to follow their dreams. Hadn't she, herself, when she left Moonbeam and concentrated on her art and her illustrations? Okay, that might have been more of a running away thing than a chasing thing. But, still.

Heather strolled along the shops on the wharf, popping into a few of them to see if much had changed. There was a new store with a fabulous selection of teas and coffees. The same old t-shirt and beach decor shops that had always been there—even if a few of them had new names. A few of the shops carried prints of some of her work with signs proclaiming they were from a local artist.

Heather Parker. After she moved out and started illustrating, she hadn't wanted to use her real last name, Carlson, on her art. Whether it was that her father had been so against her *silly, childish, foolish* art or what, she wasn't sure. But she took Parker as her name for her work.

Eventually, she legally changed her name... not that she'd told anyone here in Moonbeam that part. Especially her mother. But the Parker name suited her. She'd come from a long line of strong women starting with Grace Parker, who'd helped her husband open up Parker's General Store. She felt like it was some kind of homage to Grace's strength and perseverance. Besides, most of the town referred to her and Liv, as well as their moms, as the Parker women.

She stood in front of a framed print of her work, a steaming mug of coffee with a cute coffee-themed saying the company had come up with. A local artist sticker hung from the frame. She might have been born and raised in Moonbeam, but she didn't really consider herself local anymore. More of an occasional visitor. Even if she did still keep the condo and claimed it as her permanent residence. Not that anything about her life was permanent. But it was nice to see some of her work hanging here in the shops.

Hanging *anywhere*.

As far as she knew, her parents didn't have even one print of her work in their house. It didn't fit into the modern style in their home. They'd hired a fancy interior designer who planned every piece of furniture, every rug, every piece of home decor accessory. But still, it stung just a tiny bit. But mostly she ignored it. Or tried to. She knew that both Aunt Donna and Livy had some of her work displayed in their homes.

"Heather, dear." Jackie and Jillian Jenkins interrupted her thoughts. "You're back in town. So good to see you."

She glanced around quickly and realized she couldn't avoid the two town busybodies. Sisters. Spinsters, if that was still even a term. Neither had married, they lived together in the house they were raised in, and they knew everything about everyone... and weren't afraid to spread any tiny tidbit of news or scandal. To top that off they were twins, and for the life of her she wasn't sure who was who.

"Hi." She pasted on a smile.

"You haven't been home in a while," Jackie said.

Or at least she *thought* it was Jackie. She bet they knew how long she'd been gone down to the day. "It has been a while."

"You know, Jackie and I were just talking about you."

Ha, the other twin spoke so she'd been right to guess the first one was Jackie. "Oh?"

"Yes. We were wondering if you were ever going to settle down. You must get tired of all the travel."

"I love all the travel," she corrected Jillian. And she did love the travel. Loved to see new places. Usually.

"Your father's been out of town a long time this time," Jackie jumped in.

"Oh." If she kept giving them 'oh' answers would they leave her alone?

"Yes, a very long time this time."

"He travels a lot with his business." She didn't know why she was defending his absence. She was *glad* he was gone while she was in town.

"He's gone a lot." Jillian bobbed her head. "Leaving your poor momma all alone. And you rarely come home either."

She glanced at her watch. "Oh, look at the time. I'm going to be late. It was so nice to see you both." Nothing like a bald-faced lie to start her day.

She turned away and hurried down to the end of the pier, glancing over at the marina. The Destiny was tied to her slip at the end of the second long dock that extended out over the

47

water. Jesse Brown. She hadn't thought about him in years.

As if her thoughts had conjured him up from the depths of her memories, she saw him coming down the lengthy dock, his face tanned, his legs stretching out in long strides.

She stepped back into the shadows by the last shop. Not hiding from him. Not really. She watched as he turned and headed the other direction. When he was far enough away, she walked back out into the sunlight and headed in the opposite direction than Jesse had taken. Even though she *had* planned on going in his direction to her mother's house, but not now.

Not after the huge fight she and Jesse had the very last time she saw him. Even Livy didn't know about that.

Heather took the long way to her mother's house to avoid Jesse and slowly walked up the long circle drive. Maybe her mother wouldn't be here and she could just leave a message with the housekeeper that she'd stopped by... She sighed. But if that happened, she'd still have to make time to come see her later.

She rang the doorbell and her mother opened the door, surprise showing on her face. "Oh... Heather."

Equal surprise probably showed on her own face at her mother answering the door instead of the housekeeper.

"Hi, Mom." She walked past her mother into the impressive two-story foyer. She glanced over at the large stack of boxes against one wall in the usually spotless foyer. "What's that?"

"Oh... nothing. Just getting rid of a few things."

She didn't miss the slight look of guilt on her mother's face. Maybe her mom felt guilty about all the stuff she bought and now was trying to dispose of. All the things that she just *had* to have. The constant shopping expeditions. The paintings and art pieces precisely placed in the house. The furniture that was never the same any time she came to visit. Really, how many times could one person replace a couch?

"I was nearby and I thought I'd stop by." She got the distinct feeling her mother wasn't very thrilled about her visit. And yet, hadn't her mother looked like her feelings had been hurt when she saw her at the wharf with Liv and hadn't known she was in town? "Do you want me to come back another time?"

Her mother's look rested briefly on the tower of boxes. "No, of course not. I'm glad to see you. Come have some tea out on the patio with me. Go on out. I'll get the tea."

Heather walked through the foyer into the great room and out through one of the numerous French doors leading outside. The view across the bay always made her pause. It truly was a beautiful view. She missed watching the sunsets from her upstairs bedroom she'd had at the house when she'd lived here. That had been one of the few things she loved about moving here. She loved watching the brilliant colors illuminate the sky, then dim into nothingness as the stars came out to twinkle over the bay. Her parents were lucky to have this view. Not that she remembered them sitting out and enjoying it often. They weren't really outside people.

She turned to see her mother coming out with a tray with a pitcher of tea, glasses full of ice, a small plate of lemon slices, and another plate of some kind of fancy pastries. She might let the cook put dinner on the table and the housekeeper run the house, but her mother knew how to bake. She was always making some kind of scrumptious recipe, usually one passed down for generations in their family. Alas, she hadn't inherited the baking gene from her mother.

Her mother sank gracefully down on a chair and she plopped down on a seat beside her with recently recovered cushions—she was certain this was a new pattern than last time she was here—and picked up her glass of sweet tea.

"So, are you here for long this time?" her mother asked in her perfect polite-society voice.

"I'm not sure. For a while." She looked over at her mom. "Is... is Father here?"

Her mother averted her eyes, suddenly very interested in her tea. "Ah... no. He's away."

She hid her sigh of relief. The last thing she wanted was to run into her father.

"When is he returning?" If she was smart and lucky, she'd get out of Moonbeam before then.

"I— I'm not certain."

She frowned slightly. That wasn't like her mother. Her mother had a planner and things written in it at least a year out. She always knew exactly when her father was returning and no doubt had planned a half-dozen social dinners for them.

"So, where are you headed next?" Her mother changed the subject.

"I'm not sure. Maybe a cabin in the mountains for a bit. Do some hiking." She had in mind a series of illustrations of a woman hiking in the mountains, sitting by streams, sitting on the front porch of a cabin. The character would be reading. Enjoying herself. Discovering nature. Different than her usual beachy illustrations.

As usual, her mother made no mention of her art, nor did she ask any questions about it. Fine. That was fine by her. Really fine. Just very, very fine.

She set her tea down and the ice cubes rattled against the sides of the glass. "I can't stay long..."

"That's okay. I have a meeting I need to go to soon."

That sounded more like her mother. Probably arranging some event with The Ladies Club. Planning a charity gala. Arranging catering for a party. Her mother was nothing if not the master at planning events.

She stood. "Well, I should let you get to it then."

Her mother rose gracefully from her chair. "I'm glad you stopped by. Will I see you again before you leave town?"

"Sure, Mom. I'm sure you will." She headed down the stairs off the patio to the walkway around the outside of the house. She looked back just before she turned the corner and saw her mother just standing there on the expansive patio, looking out at the bay.

Her mother didn't seem like herself today. But then, she didn't really know her mother anymore, did she?

CHAPTER 6

Olivia looked up and smiled as a new customer walked up to the malt shop counter. "Good afternoon."

He slid onto the stool. "Now *you* must be the Livy my friend Del was telling me about. And I met your mother, Donna, when I was here yesterday."

She didn't recognize him from being in here before or from around town. "I am Livy. Glad to see you back so soon."

He gave her a warm smile. "I'm Barry. I'm working on The Cabot Hotel. Discovered your ice cream yesterday and I'm afraid it's going to be the downfall of my diet."

"Ah. So Delbert told you about my family's secret recipe best-ever ice cream, right?" She smiled back, automatically pulled in by his friendliness.

"He did. I was in yesterday and your mother made me a vanilla malt. Think I'll try a chocolate one today."

"I'm warning you, our ice cream is addictive." She tossed him a grin as she turned to make his malt.

Her mother came up to the counter. "Well, hello there, neighbor."

Olivia turned around from her malt-making. "Neighbor?"

"Barry rented the Meyer's house."

"And your mother walked me home when I got just a *bit* turned around last night."

"Oh, I see." She looked from her mother to Barry. Interesting. Her mother hadn't mentioned anything about a handsome man renting the house next to her. Nor the fact that she'd walked home with him.

She turned back, finished making the malt, and handed it to Barry. "Here you go. Enjoy." She turned to her mother. "Oh, I invited Heather to go with us to Pelican Cay. I hope that's okay."

"Of course it is." Her mother turned to Barry. "We're taking my boat over to Pelican

Cay on Saturday. There's a beautiful beach there. Not many people because the island is only reachable by boat. The water turns into this amazing shade of crystal clear turquoise out there. It's a little chilly for swimming this time of year, but it's perfect for beach walking and shelling."

"Sounds beautiful."

Olivia couldn't quite read her mother's expression—probably because it shifted three or four times in as many seconds, as though acting out whatever war was raging in her thoughts. One side must have won because her mother smiled at Barry. "So... would you like to join us?"

Ah, so that was what she was warring with. Wondering whether to invite her new neighbor.

"I—are you sure I wouldn't be intruding?" Barry looked between Olivia and her mother.

"Not at all," her mother insisted.

"Please join us," she added to her mother's invite. Hey, if her mother wanted to invite some man to go with them, more power to her. Maybe she was just being neighborly, but maybe not. There was a bit of sparkle to her eyes when she spoke to Barry. Interesting...

"Great. Then I'd love to go." He gave her mother a warm smile. A *very* warm smile.

"Meet us at my dock at nine on Saturday. I'm packing us all a picnic."

"Can I bring anything?"

"Nope, I've got it all under control. We'll see you then." Her mother hurried off to help a group of customers entering the shop.

Hm... this turn of events was certainly different. She'd have to keep an eye on her mother. See if there was anything going on between her and this Barry guy. Not that she minded if there was. Her mother rarely dated. She'd dated Stan Winkleman off and on years ago. Like lots of years ago. Stan had fallen by the wayside about the time Emily was born. Her mother had been so busy with the shop and helping raise Emily. She guessed Stan had gotten tired of too many no-I'm-busys back then.

Saturday was looking like it would be an interesting trip. She smiled to herself as she went to wait on another customer.

CHAPTER 7

Donna checked the boat on Saturday morning to make sure everything was set for their outing. She'd packed a large rolling cooler with their picnic. The weather was warm for a winter's day, but she still wore a light jacket. People always imagined that southern Florida had hot summery days all year long, but in the winter she did have to occasionally wear jeans and sweaters. She should have thought to tell Barry to bring a jacket. It got kind of breezy this time of year on the bay.

And why *had* she invited Barry? She hardly knew him. She'd tried hard to convince herself that she was just being neighborly. That was all this was. She'd *almost* convinced herself. Almost.

She glanced up as she heard laughter and

saw Olivia, Emily, and Heather approaching the dock. Barry trailed not far behind them.

"Hey, Heather, this is Barry. Mom's neighbor for a bit," Olivia said. "And, Barry, have you met my daughter, Emily?"

"Not formally. Saw her at Parker's, though. Nice to meet both of you." He turned to Donna. "I brought a jacket. Figured it might get chilly on the boat ride."

"It might." She nodded. "All of you come aboard. Let's get this outing started."

She hugged Heather as she climbed aboard. "So glad you're home for a bit and could join us. We've missed you."

"I missed you all, too. Can't wait to get out on the beach." Heather hugged her back, then headed to the bow.

The girls all grabbed seats near the bow. Barry came back by the captain's seat... which was really a bench. A small bench, but big enough for two if they sat close. Very close.

"Mind if I join you here?" He nodded at the seat.

"Yes. I mean, no." She shook her head at her foolishness. Why was she suddenly so nervous? "Yes, join me." There, that was better.

He slid onto the bench beside her and she

smelled the fresh scent of a woodsy aftershave. His arm bumped against hers and she tucked hers close to her side.

She maneuvered them away from the dock, and they wandered through the canal system at a slow speed. She turned to Barry. "Minimum wake through the waterways to prevent damage to the seawalls, and it helps protect the manatees, too. We're about twenty minutes from the inlet that leads to the bay at this speed."

"This is just fascinating to me. I've never been somewhere like this." He looked all around as they slid past expensive mansions with tiny original homes tucked between them.

Almost all were well kept and each beautiful in its own way. Many had pool cages over their pools to protect from the bugs. This time of year she loved to have all her sliders opened to the caged area. It made the house feel so expansive.

"Years ago, they dug out the land and made the canal system. The original part is up near the bay, near the downtown area. Then they added this part, also years ago—my grandparents built the house I live in—and the town kept expanding into new areas. South of us there's a brand new area that's booming with new homes and a smattering of condos, but I really like this older area the best."

"I'd never find my way back to your house through the canals with all the twists and turns we've made."

She smiled. "I grew up here so it's all imprinted on my brain. It takes a bit to learn the ways out to the bay for newcomers, I'm sure."

They slid through the waterways until they reached the outlet to the bay. As they got past the channel markers, she increased their speed and they slipped across the waters toward the small islands that dotted the entrance to the bay and lined the gulf near Moonbeam.

She'd heard all the arguments that they weren't really on the ocean, or technically not on the sea. Moonbeam Bay was on the Gulf of Mexico. But it didn't matter to her. It was ocean as far as she was concerned.

She steered them out across the bay, ignoring the fact that Barry sat right against her, leaning close to ask questions over the noise of the motor and the wind. She pulled up to a dock on the bay side of the island and Olivia scampered out to tie them up.

"In the summer, we usually just anchor on the beach side and wade ashore. But it's a bit chilly for that now. So, we'll take the boardwalk across the island, it's not far," she explained to Barry.

He helped swing the cooler with their picnic up onto the dock. Its large wheels made it easier to pull across the boardwalk and beach. Olivia gathered the large bag with the beach blankets, Heather grappled with the beach umbrella, and Emily grabbed a small bucket for her shelling.

The girls walked at a faster pace and soon pulled away from where she and Barry walked, tugging the cooler along with them. Soon the waters of the gulf came into view.

"Oh, look. A blue heron." She pointed to where the large bird made his majestic flight above them.

Barry paused and shielded his eyes from the sun, watching the bird as it landed at the edge of the water in front of them. "Impressive bird."

"They are. One of my favorites." Though she had lots of favorite birds. The blue herons. The very pelicans this island was named after. The bright red cardinals. She loved going to the nearby wildlife area and birdwatching. Well, she used to. Back when she had time for things like that. She frowned slightly, wondering when she'd last gone and making a mental note to plan an outing there soon.

They got to the sand and tugged the cooler across to where the girls had spread out a couple of blankets and stuck the umbrella in the ground in case they needed a spot of shade.

"Mom, Emily's already off down the beach shelling. Heather and I are going to head that way and catch up with her."

She nodded at Olivia and dropped onto the worn, much-used beach blanket. The warmth of the sun seeped through her and she shrugged off her jacket. Barry sank onto the blanket beside her and slipped his off too.

"Can't ask for better weather than this. Hard to believe it's winter. I'm not complaining about lack of shoveling snow or the lack of needing a winter coat." He gave her an easy smile.

A smile that somehow relaxed her and made her a bit edgy at the same time. So she concentrated on ignoring it. "I do love winters here. There are more people and traffic this time of year. The tourists flock here to avoid those winters, but it just brings in more business to the town. It's good for the economy." She laughed. "And the tourists do seem to like ice cream and then explore the general store. Win-win."

"And if they're anything like me, they'll come back daily for ice cream while they're in town." He gave her that easy, trouble-free smile again, and she shifted restlessly beside him.

Olivia walked at the water's edge with Heather. The water chilled her bare feet but wasn't unbearable. It felt almost like old times with her cousin here walking beside her. Heather paused and picked up a shell, leaned over and rinsed it in the water, and tucked it in her pocket.

"One more for your collection?" Olivia teased.

"I just picked up this pretty antique glass vase at that new secondhand shop that opened in town. I thought I might fill it with shells."

"You already have a half dozen or more containers of shells at your condo. You realize that, right?" She laughed. "But, what's one more? You should probably double down on your efforts of collecting them today."

"What can I say? I love to go shelling."

"Then you should come home more often

and go shelling with me. I miss you when you're away."

"Home." Heather paused. "I... I don't really feel like I have a home anymore."

The sentence tore at Olivia's heart. "Oh, Heather. Of course, you do. Moonbeam will always be your home."

Heather shrugged. "I don't know. My condo doesn't feel like a home. And Moonbeam... sometimes it doesn't feel like home anymore, either. I feel like a fraud when the stores label me as a local artist when they sell my prints."

She stood next to Heather not failing to miss the loneliness in her cousin's voice. She grabbed Heather's hand and squeezed it. "Why don't you move back here? You don't need to travel around so much now, do you? You could buy a place that you love and make it feel like home. You know I'd love having you back here."

"And I'd love seeing you more. But I've moved on... why would I come back?"

"Don't be silly. You have me and Em. You have Mom. And you have your mother... even though I know that whole relationship is... difficult. And..." She stopped, wondering if she was brave enough to go on. She plunged ahead. "And your father isn't here much.

There's no reason to let him chase you away anymore."

Heather looked out at the blue water of the gulf. "I— I don't know. I just don't know."

"You should at least think about it."

Heather turned back, sadness etched on her features. "I don't think... I don't think I'm strong enough to move back."

"Hey, Heather, look at this cool shell." Emily hurried up to them before Olivia could assure Heather that of course she was strong enough.

Heather's face slipped into a reluctant, if not totally convincing, smile. "Here, Em, let me see."

The three of them headed back toward the beach blankets, Emily and Heather pausing frequently to pick up shells. She smiled at their shared love of beachcombing, always looking for that interesting find. It was nice to have Heather here. She'd just work on getting her cousin to stay this time. At least she'd try...

They got to the blankets and Emily plopped down. "I'm starving."

"Of course you are." Olivia knelt beside her daughter and opened the cooler. "You always are."

She passed out the sandwiches and drinks

her mom had made, along with a container of fresh fruit and another one of cookies.

"So Donna tells me you work at Parker's, right?" Barry asked Emily.

"I do. And I work at the history museum part-time. I love it. There is so much history to this area and the whole state." Emily set down her soda. "Like that old hotel. Mom said you were in town to manage restoring it. The hotel has a fascinating past."

Emily's eyes lit up when she talked about the history of the area. Emily had always loved learning everything about the past, in this area and worldwide.

"Do they have books about the hotel's history at the museum?" Barry asked.

"We do. We sell quite a few books about the history of the area. It helps fund the museum."

"I should check them out. Del tried to keep the hotel as close to its origins as possible. You know, with updated wiring and plumbing." He grinned.

Emily laughed. "You should stop by then. We're at Third and Magnolia. Do you know where that is?"

"Strangely, I do. I believe I got lost there this

week." Barry smiled. "But Donna kindly rescued me."

As Barry chatted with Emily, he kept glancing at Donna. If Olivia's instincts were correct, he was interested in her mom. He'd have to make some obvious move toward her, though, because her mother sure wouldn't make one toward him. He'd have to ask her out, act interested. Heck, he'd probably have to spell it out for her. Her mother was no expert on dating.

Or maybe... she could give them a little nudge.

"Barry, I hate to impose..." *But she really didn't.* "But since Em is so interested in the hotel and its history. Do you think she and I could come see it while you're working on restoring it? Mom, you'd love to see it, too, wouldn't you?" She turned to her mother and gave her an innocent look.

"Oh... well, yes. I suppose I would."

Emily jumped up dumping her pail of shells in her exuberance. "I'd *love* to see it. Can we? Please, Mr. Richmond?"

"Call me Barry. And I don't see why not."

"Grams, you want to go, too. Don't you?

Didn't you say you used to go there when you were young? Before it closed down?"

"You were once there, too. We got you ice cream from their ice cream shop by the bay, and you sat outside eating the cone until you dropped it and started crying," Olivia informed her daughter. "But Grams bought you another scoop."

"I don't remember that."

"You were really young. It was right before it closed down." Olivia smiled at the memory. It would be nice to have the hotel open again. She had good memories of going there herself as a young girl.

Barry turned to Heather. "Would you like to come, too?"

"I would." Heather nodded. "I'm happy it's going to open again."

"How does tomorrow afternoon work for everyone? The workers won't be back until Monday so it won't be so noisy."

"That sounds perfect." Olivia looked over at her mother and Heather who both nodded.

"Great," Barry said, then frowned slightly. "So, since the three generations of Parker descendants are here today and you're coming to The Cabot Hotel tomorrow, who's running the store?"

"That would be the Keating boys. They work one weekend a month so we can get a break, and help out at other times, too," Donna explained.

Olivia laughed at Barry's expression. "No doubt you're picturing two young kids running the store. The Keating brothers are in their sixties. Retired. They've always been known as the Keating boys, though. Almost as if they're one person. I don't know. Just a quirk of our town, I guess. Anyway, they like working in the store for a change every now and again. They worked there when they were teenagers. Moved on to their careers, then came back asking for part-time work to keep busy after they both retired."

"Speaking of which. We should probably pack up and head back home. I do want to pop into the store and make sure everything is going well." Her mother stood.

"Mom, you're supposed to be taking the day off."

"And I did, didn't I?" she insisted. "Well, mostly."

Mostly. Even when her mom took a day off,

she usually found a reason to pop back into the store. When was the last time her mother had a day when she didn't once step into Parker's? She frowned as she stood and brushed the sand from her legs, gathering up items to put back into the cooler.

Maybe she'd just make it her mission to see that her mother took a full day off.

She laughed to herself. She'd probably have about as much luck with that as she was going to have convincing Heather to move back to Moonbeam.

CHAPTER 8

Barry waved to Olivia, Emily, and Heather as they left the dock. He turned to help Donna with the cooler. "Here, let me get that." He swung it onto the dock.

Donna checked the boat, climbed off, and put the lift up, suspending the boat over the canal water. He nodded at the lift. "Those are different than what we had on a lake near us when I was growing up. The boats there were on lifts that float on pontoon-like supports."

"These are used here because of the changes in the tides, suspending the boats from cables." Donna pointed across the lake to a large trawler. "Though some larger boats are kept just tied up to their dock, and not on lifts."

"Not really a boater myself, but I sure enjoyed going out today."

"I learned my way around a boat probably about the time I could walk." Donna's eyes sparkled as she laughed. "My grandfather would set me and my sister on his knees and let us steer his boat. Anyway, been boating ever since. At least when I make time for it."

"Speaking of making time. Could I repay you for your kind invite by making you dinner tonight? I could grill out some burgers for us?"

Indecision flitted across her face.

"I really do need to check on the store."

"That would give me time to run get groceries." He waited for her reply, suddenly not wanting to spend his evening all alone.

"How about this? You get the makings for burgers, and I'll make us salad to go with them. We can grill at my place. You can see the view. It looks like it will be a spectacular sunset with all the clouds in the sky." She laughed. "Unless they all dissipate. You just never know."

"Okay. That sounds like a plan. I'll be over about five-thirty? Does that work?"

"It does."

He pulled the cooler up to her house, then

picked it up, following her inside and placing it down on the tile floor of the kitchen. He looked around the room. The walls were a light neutral almost white while the cabinets were stained a warm gray color. She had pops of teal and yellow in the kitchen that followed through to items scattered around the great room. Large windows encased the showy view of the lake created by the convergence of a smattering of canals.

A small pool and spa were enclosed by a large pool cage, and an expansive lanai with tables, chairs, and chaise lounges stretched out from a sliding door off the kitchen. A wonderful, homey house. "Your home is just... charming." He couldn't think of a better word to describe it.

Donna blushed a lovely shade of rose. "Thank you. I did make some changes after it became mine. Lightened the wall color. Restained the dark cabinets to this lighter gray color. I find I like doing the work myself. I'm always working on some kind of rehab project."

"Really?" He couldn't remember if he'd ever so much as fixed something, which now that he thought about it was strange since he oversaw so much reconstruction. He'd never painted anything. Never lived anywhere long enough to need to paint anything. "Well, I'm impressed by your skills."

"Oh, just things my grandfather taught me how to do. Evelyn—that's my sister—and I spent lots of time here with our grandparents. Our parents traveled around a lot. Some for my father's work, some just for pleasure. But my grandparents were always glad to let us stay here with them. I think I might have spent more time here than at my parents' house." She shrugged. "Not complaining. Loved staying here with them."

"And your parents? They're gone?" He didn't know how to ask the question, exactly. Asking if they were dead seemed harsh. Dead was such a hard word.

"My father... he passed away last year."

"I'm sorry."

"Ah, yes." Donna turned and placed a tote bag on the counter. "Thanks."

Her tone was careful, measured, as though giving the reply that was expected but not heartfelt.

"Mother lives in a retirement place in Naples. She's off on a world tour with a group of ladies from there. I guess she's having fun. Haven't heard much from her on the trip."

She seemed to have a dispassionate vibe about not hearing from her mother. There was more to the story here, that much he could tell. But it wasn't his way to pry. He'd asked enough questions.

"I'm off, then. I'll see you this evening?"

She walked him through the house to the front door. "Bye."

He walked over to the small house he was renting. When he glanced back, he saw Donna standing in the doorway, watching him. That Donna Foster was an interesting woman and she intrigued him. He waved, then unlocked the door and slipped inside.

Donna checked on Parker's, but the Keating brothers had everything under control and chased her away, assuring her things were going well and they expected to *not* see her tomorrow. She went back home and set the table on the lanai for two. A strange number for her. It was usually just for one... and truth be told, she often just ate standing at the counter in the kitchen.

And if she did set the table out here, it was for three when Olivia and Emily would join her.

She placed white plates on sunny, yellow placemats with multi-colored cloth napkins. She grabbed the teal solar lantern from its place in the sun and placed it on the table for light after the sunset.

After fluffing the pillows on the chairs and glancing around to make sure everything at least looked picked up, she hurried inside to change clothes. She stood in front of her large closet and stared into the abyss of familiarity. She'd basically worn the same size for years... and some of her clothes had been in this very same closet all that time. How could a woman have all these clothes, yet nothing to wear? Olivia was always offering to take her shopping, and now she wished she'd taken her daughter up it at least once. All her clothing was so... dated.

She finally decided on a pale yellow top and a pair of soft gray slacks. She pulled her hair back and twisted it into a bun, though a few locks escaped. Glancing in the mirror, she hoped it came across as casual-chic and not messy-disheveled.

She returned to the kitchen and made the

salad, then looked around the room and put away some items that had accumulated on the counter until the kitchen looked all picked up. At the sound of a knock, she quickly hung up a kitchen towel and went to answer the door.

She caught a glance of her reflection in the mirror by the door and tucked a flyaway hair behind her ear, still hoping for the casual-chic look. When she opened the door, Barry stood there, his arms laden with packages. A cloth bag of groceries, a bottle of wine tucked under his arm, and a bouquet of flowers in his other hand.

"For you." He handed her the flowers.

"Thank you." She motioned him inside and led him to the kitchen. When was the last time anyone had given her flowers? She couldn't remember. A very long time. The simple gesture pleased her. Pleased her more than she could say.

Barry set the bag and the wine on the counter. "I went ahead and made up the burgers, and I got some buns from the bakery, and... well, they had peach pie and I couldn't resist. So I got us some slices."

"Perfect." She hadn't even thought of

making a dessert. Besides, she was a so-so baker, not an expert like Evelyn.

She arranged the flowers in a mason jar, admiring their simple beauty. Daises, white and yellow carnations, and a few bunches of baby's breath. "They really are pretty. Thank you."

"My pleasure." Barry glanced out to the lanai. "Let me open the wine, then should I start the grill?"

"Sure. It's gas. Should be all ready to go."

She handed him the wine opener, and he deftly uncorked the red wine. Then he walked outside and lit the grill, glancing back toward her once and smiling.

It seemed... strange. Strange to have a man here doing such simple things as opening wine for her and starting the grill. She was always the one in charge. The one opening wine. Starting the grill. Cooking.

He came back inside and poured wine into the two glasses she'd placed on the counter. He handed one to her and their fingers brushed. She looked quickly up into his eyes, and he was staring right back. Then a brief smile crept over his lips. "Ah, it's nice out. Should we sit outside while the grill heats up?"

She cleared her throat. "Yes, let's."

They moved outside and settled onto two lounge chairs, facing the view out over Sunset Lake. Silence hung between them. She debated if it was a comfortable silence or an awkward one...

Just talk to her. Say something.

Barry silently commanded himself, not sure why he was so tongue-tied all of a sudden. He tried again. "Ah, it's a nice evening. And your view is nice. It does look like we'll have a *nice* sunset." *Nice, nice, nice.* What was wrong with him?

"It is a pleasant evening. I love this time of year. Well, I love all times of the year except maybe the dead of summer when it rains all the time and the humidity skyrockets. But even then, I'm okay with it. Wouldn't want to live anywhere else."

"So you've lived here your whole life?"

"I have."

"I can't imagine that. I've lived... everywhere. Truly. I mostly just travel from job to job. I have a small apartment in Chicago. I'm rarely there, though. Mostly just a mailing address."

"Any family?"

"Ah... no. I'm an only child. And both my parents are gone."

"I'm sorry."

"It was years ago. I was a bit of a—how should I say this—*surprise* to them later in life. They were thrilled though. They were great parents. They both died when I was just out of college, though."

"No aunts or uncles? Cousins?"

"Afraid not. It's just me." He shrugged and took a sip of his wine. And usually, it didn't bother him that it was just him. Usually. But today, seeing Donna with Olivia and Emily, it did make his lone existence seem a bit... *lonely*, empty, isolated. And Donna had her mom, her sister, and her niece. And who knew who else? Not to mention a lifetime of friends from growing up in this town.

"Did you ever marry?" She interrupted his thoughts.

"Ah, no. Almost. Once. But... it didn't work out." He looked over at her. "And you?"

"I was married once. To Olivia's father. He... left. Didn't like living here in Moonbeam, didn't like how his life changed when we had a child. He left when she was about two."

"That must have been hard for you." He couldn't imagine raising a child alone.

"It was..." She shrugged. "It was what it was. I had no choice. I had my job at Parker's, and my grandmother helped me with Olivia."

He noticed she said her grandmother helped her, not her mother.

"Do you ever see him? Does he come see Olivia and Emily?" He was curious about this man who left Donna—a totally charming woman as far as he was concerned—and her young daughter.

"No. He's never seen Emily, and she's sixteen now. I think the last time he was here was over twenty years ago." She looked out over the water. "But his loss. He missed out on knowing two great young women."

"They do seem like exceptional young women. I really enjoyed our outing today." He stood. "Let me go grab the burgers and get them on the grill."

He came back and grilled their dinner while they chatted of less serious topics. The new restaurant on the wharf. The best place to get fresh seafood. The weather for the upcoming week. Safe topics. He was fine with safe topics. Safe topics were *nice*.

They ate their dinner, then moved to two Adirondack chairs out on the point as the sun dipped behind the palm trees on the far side of the lake. A lone sailboat slipped by under power, returning from a trip to the harbor, its sail down and stored. The sky darkened from pale yellow, to orange, to purple in an amazing kaleidoscope of color as the last of the sunset faded away.

"That was remarkable," he said as the stars began to poke out of the darkness above him. "I can't remember the last time I've just sat and watched a sunset."

Her voice drifted over in a small laugh. "I do as often as I can. At least a couple times a week I sit out here and watch it. It's my... happy time, I guess. So peaceful. Such a simple pleasure and it brings me so much joy."

He looked over at her profile in the soft evening light. He admired how she just appreciated such a simple, ordinary moment like a sunset. How she made time to come out and watch them.

Truth be told, there was a lot he admired about this woman. He raised his glass in a silent salute to her, to the sunset, to the moment. Her lips curled into a smile, unaware of what a captivating picture she made with that smile and her wisps of hair floating around her face in the breeze. She raised her glass and they both took a sip, savoring the moment.

CHAPTER 9

Donna had arranged to meet Olivia, Emily, and Heather at The Cabot Hotel. Olivia laughed and called her out on stopping by Parker's on the way. Which is exactly what she did. Everything was fine there, of course. The Keatings had everything under control.

She walked through the opened doors of the hotel and heard voices. She followed the voices to find the girls standing in the doorway out to the back porch facing the bay. She hurried up to join them.

Barry turned as she approached, a wide, welcoming smile on his face. "Donna, there you are. Good. We were just going out to see the view."

As she walked past him, he briefly touched

her elbow and steered her outside. A simple gesture, yet... somehow it delighted her. Which was silly, of course.

"I'd forgotten how beautiful it is here." Heather looked out over the water in appreciation.

"Me, too. I can just imagine staying at the hotel and having a drink out here on the porch and watching the sunset." Donna looked out at the boats gliding through the waters of the bay. Some headed out to the gulf, some heading up the river that flowed into the harbor. The breeze blew her hair into her eyes, and she reached up to grab it in one hand to pull it back.

She caught Barry staring at her and looked quickly away, pretending she hadn't noticed.

"When will you have the hotel ready to open?" Emily asked. "I can't wait to see it all finished. Are you going to have a grand opening?"

Barry laughed at all her questions. "Hoping to open in a few more months. Maybe three? Hadn't thought about a grand opening."

"I think a grand opening party is a great idea." Delbert Hamilton came walking out onto the deck.

"Del, thought you were out of town for a bit longer." Barry shook Del's hand.

"I was supposed to, but Camille planned a party over on Belle Island and wants me there. You know, duty calls."

Del didn't look too thrilled about his duty, but that was none of Donna's business. She assumed Camille was his girlfriend?

Del turned to Olivia and Emily. "Good afternoon, ladies. And who is this?"

"This is Heather, my cousin," Olivia answered.

"Nice to meet you, Heather." Del gave her a warm smile.

"We were talking about the hotel yesterday, and Emily here works at the history museum. Knew some interesting facts about the hotel, so I invited them to come see it," Barry explained.

"I've seen you working at Parker's, but you work at the history museum, too?" Del's eyes lit up. "And you know about the hotel?"

Emily nodded. "I've been researching it some while I'm working at the museum."

"Ah, that's fabulous. I found a whole storeroom of albums and memorabilia from days gone by here at the hotel. I'd actually been planning on a kind of history of the hotel with photos and displays in the library room off of the lobby."

"Oh, that's a cool idea." Emily nodded enthusiastically.

"I need someone who's interested in… well, to sort through everything and put things together for the room. Is that something you'd be interested in?"

"Are you kidding? I'd love to do that." Emily practically hopped up and down.

Donna smiled at Emily's eagerness and energy. The girl did love her history.

"That's perfect. I could show you the room now, then you could come and sort through things when it fits in your schedule. I know you must be busy with two jobs and school."

"We can adjust her workload at Parker's so she has time for this," Donna assured him. "I'm sure it's something she'd really enjoy."

"I'll pay you a fair wage, of course."

"You'll pay me to do it?" Emily's eyes widened. "Heck, I'd do it for free. It's so cool."

They all laughed and Delbert smiled. "Of course, I'll pay you. And it will be nice to have someone with knowledge of the hotel that I can ask questions of. Let me show you the room."

"I'll be back, Mom. Okay?"

Olivia nodded and turned to Donna as Emily and Del walked away. "Well, that's a job right up Emily's alley. She'll be thrilled to sort through all those pieces of the past."

"Well, I'm grateful. I know Del had all that in storage and I was hoping he wasn't wanting me to sort through it all. Much better someone who knows a bit about the town and the hotel." Barry turned to her. "You sure you can spare her from Parker's? I hate to steal her way."

"We'll be fine," Donna said.

"Mind if Heather and I go upstairs and peek in some of the guest rooms?" Olivia asked.

"Go right ahead. The ones on the top floor are mostly finished. The second floor, not so much."

"Okay, thanks. We'll be back soon," Heather said as she and Olivia hurried off to the main stairway.

Barry turned back to her. "Want to poke around or sit and enjoy the view?"

"Let's sit for a few minutes." She sat down on the top step of the wide wooden porch and Barry settled beside her.

"Going to put some Adirondack chairs out here and a few gliders. I want this porch to be a place people can sit and chat and drink and just enjoy the view."

"I predict this hotel will be a smashing success when it's opened again. I'm glad Del bought it and is giving it the care it deserves." She glanced down the long porch, noticing random new planks put down here and there. The workers had been busy fixing things up. "I've missed the hotel. Missed coming here. And Moonbeam is always grateful for another attraction to bring people to town. Tourism keeps the town going."

"I hope it is successful. It was a shame to let this fine place just sit empty."

"Not to mention the clamoring that had started to tear it down." She sighed. "But it couldn't just stay here empty forever."

"Well, now it won't. We just need to finish the rehabbing and she'll be open again and filled with people."

"Oh, look." Donna pointed out at the bay. "The Destiny. See, that large, two-level boat? It's owned by a local man, Jesse Brown. Depending on the day it takes sunrise cruises or cruises out to Pelican Cay where we were yesterday. And then at night on the weekends, it has a dinner cruise to see the sunset."

"I've seen it go past here. Wondered what it was."

"Jesse's a fine young man. Went to school with Heather and Olivia."

"I'll have to see if I can fit one of his dinner cruises into my schedule. Maybe you could join me?" Barry cocked his head when he asked the question.

"I... uh... Sure. Maybe we could work that out." Had he just asked her out on a date? She wasn't certain. She looked away and rolled her eyes at herself, so out of practice on this dating thing. *If* this was a dating thing...

Olivia peeked out the French door on one of the grand suites on the upper floor of The Cabot. "The view here is spectacular."

"So is this whole suite. Did you see how nice they've done everything? It would be fabulous to stay here, almost like a throw-back to earlier times." Heather walked up beside her to take in the view.

"Hey, there's Jesse's boat. See it?" Olivia pointed.

"Oh, is it?" Heather answered noncommittally.

But Olivia ignored her cousin's meager attempt at subterfuge. "Yes. You know, we should go on a dinner cruise while you're here. See what all he's done to the old boat. I hear it's really nice now. Great food. It would be fun."

"We'll see. I'm pretty busy. Have some projects that are due to be sent in soon."

"Right. We'll see." Olivia wasn't sure what was going on there. Jesse and Heather had always been good friends. She assumed Heather saw him when she came to town. Why didn't she want to go see his boat—or him, for that matter—now?

"So. Aunt Donna and Barry. You think something's going on there?" Heather changed the subject.

"I'm not sure. I mean... he seems really nice. I'd love to see Mom dating someone."

"She hasn't really dated since Stan, has she?"

"No, not often. A random date here and there. I feel like she gave up so much and devoted her life to helping me with Emily. Now I wish she'd take time for herself."

"Parker's keeps her pretty busy though, doesn't it?"

"It does. And I try to take on more of the responsibility, but she's so used to running it and doing things her own way." She shrugged. "I'd change some things, but... well, it won't ever happen."

"Have you told her this? Told her you want to do more?"

"I try, but you know Mom. She kind of agrees, but then still does it all."

"She's always been like that. I'm sometimes amazed how different Aunt Donna and Mom are. It's like they were raised in different families or something."

"They are different." Olivia turned from the view. "Oh, did you hear that Grandmother is off on a world tour?"

"I did. I guess she just needed to get away. I was sorry I didn't make it in for Grandfather's funeral."

"It was... a strange event. A lot of people I've never even met. No tears. Not by anyone. And I know it sounds horrible and strange... but I swear it was almost like Grandmother looked—" She paused, feeling guilty even finishing the sentence.

"Almost like what?" Heather prodded.

"Like she was relieved?"

"Well, Grandfather was a hard man to... uh... like."

"He was a hard man, period. Cold. But still. He was Mom and Aunt Evelyn's father and... hardly anyone from Moonbeam was there. Mostly people from their Naples retirement place and business associates of Grandfather's."

"Because he didn't really have any friends, did he? I mean, I never saw him do anything with friends. He'd golf with business associates. Go to charity events. But... did he have friends?"

She shrugged. "Not that I know of. I guess Grandmother does now. At least friendly enough to take this world cruise with. It probably did her good to get away."

All of a sudden Heather hugged her and laughed. "Livy, I think we're the most normal out of our family. I'm glad we're friends."

Olivia hugged her back. "Yes, we were lucky. We *are* lucky." She pulled away slightly. "Even if I do have to share my birthday with you."

Heather laughed again. "Hey, it's my birthday, too. Just because you were born an hour before me, it's still my day."

"I still find it strange that we were born on the same day." Olivia shook her head. "What are the odds?"

"Remember that one year when we were girls and we insisted we both were going to have our own party?"

"After years of sharing our parties? Yes, I remember."

"Our friends couldn't decide on which party to go to and didn't want to hurt the other one's feelings." Heather laughed. "So, no one came."

"To either of them." Olivia grinned. "That was the last time we made that mistake."

Olivia took Heather's arm and they headed back downstairs. Emily came rushing up to them as they reached the first floor.

"Oh, Mom. You should see all the stuff Mr. Hamilton has in that storage room. Photo albums. Paintings. Guest registers dating back from the early nineteen hundreds. There's even a couple of trunks of old clothes. Just so much cool stuff." Emily swirled around them.

Olivia laughed. "Well, sounds like you'll be busy sorting through all that."

"I'm sure it will keep her busy. I can't wait to see what we can come up with for the history area in the library," Del added and turned to Emily. "And, Emily, call me Del. Please."

"Really? Okay." Emily's eyes shone at being treated as an adult.

Her mother and Barry walked up to them. "Have you seen the ballroom? It's not finished yet, but it's starting to look like its old former glory." Barry nodded to wide doorways across the two-story lobby.

"No, can we see it?" Emily danced around them again with her usual exuberance. Olivia would like to have about a tenth of her daughter's energy at any given moment.

Barry smiled at her enthusiasm. "Sure thing." Barry and Del led them across the lobby and swung open one set of many double doors lining the wall.

Olivia gasped as they stepped inside, looking up at the three-story arched ceiling high above them. Long balconies lined each level along the sides. Huge, ornate, chandeliers hung suspended from the ceiling.

"Oh, my gosh. It's the most beautiful room I've ever seen." Emily's voice was hushed in awe.

"It is striking." Heather stepped further into the room. "I've never been in here before."

"It was closed off for years before the hotel was closed. Some structural damage to the roof. It's all been repaired now." Delbert strode into the room. "Come, come see it all. She's going to be a grand lady again. I can't wait to see people in here. Parties. Gatherings."

They all walked to the center of the room, their footsteps echoing off the tall ceiling. Olivia couldn't quit staring, her mouth open, at the grandeur of the ballroom. But at least she was in good company. Everyone stood with their necks craned staring up at the ornate ceiling above them. Light flowed through the windows lining the room, making flecks of construction dust dance in the beams of sunlight.

"Oh, I need to find some photos of this room from when they first build the hotel. We have to showcase those in the history alcove." Emily spun slowly around. "I can almost *feel* the history in here."

Her daughter was right. She could almost feel the history throbbing through her, too, if that were possible.

"It's a fine thing you're doing, Delbert, restoring this hotel," Barry said as he stood looking up at the ceiling.

Delbert beamed. "I'm pretty proud of how

it's turning out. Nothing like restoring an old hotel to its former beauty. I never get tired of it. And this one is kind of special to me."

"How come?" Emily stopped and turned toward Delbert.

"I used to come here as a boy with my grandparents. Very fond memories of the place."

"That makes the history of the hotel even that much cooler." Emily bobbed her head, her wild red curls bouncing around her shoulders. "You'll have to tell me everything you remember about it."

Delbert smiled. "I will. We'll have a long sit down and I'll tell you everything I can remember about it and then maybe, when she's all restored, she'll make magical memories for more people when they visit."

Olivia never pegged him as the romantic he was turning out to be. She had to admit, Emily's enthusiasm was catching. She, too, couldn't wait to see how all the restorations turned out and looked forward to the hotel opening again.

Donna sat out on the point that evening, sipping a glass of wine, and watching the sunset slowly slip away. She'd briefly thought of asking Barry to join her but didn't want to seem...

Seem what? She wasn't sure. Plus, he probably had things to do after they'd kept him busy all afternoon exploring the hotel. And she still was uncertain on whether he'd asked her on a date on The Destiny or maybe just meant going as neighbors.

She turned her thoughts back to the hotel. The ballroom had taken her breath away. It was stunning, even though ladders and scaffolding still lined the walls. It looked like something out of a movie set that begged for fancy dresses and orchestra music and...

She sighed. There she was getting all romantic about a room. It had been a wonderful afternoon though. She and Barry had walked home together, stopping for ice cream at Parker's on the way. Just for ice cream. Not because she was checking up on the store for the second time today.

The stars flickered above her and peace settled over the lake. Across the distance, she could hear muted laughter. A pair of pelicans swooped through the sky above her, silhouetted momentarily in the moonlight.

On a night like this, everything seemed right in her world. These moments were the ones she loved to just sit and enjoy. Wrap around her like a favorite blanket.

And yet... tonight she wished she were sharing this moment with someone else.

Her sister Evelyn.

Or Olivia and Emily.

Or... Barry.

CHAPTER 10

Olivia chased Emily out the door to school the next morning, then hurried off to Brewster's to meet Heather. They'd pretty much fallen into a routine to meet there for coffee in the mornings ever since Heather had returned. Besides, she really, *really* wanted to run something by her cousin this morning.

She had this idea. An idea that had been growing as she turned it over and over in her mind. Her logical cousin could shoot it down if it was just too crazy of an idea...

As she got to the pier, she noticed Jackie and Jillian Jenkins standing near the entrance. She quickly ducked along a side path that would take her down outside the back of the shops instead of down the wide center walkway.

She found it just good, sensible practice to avoid the sisters whenever possible. Helped keep gossip to a minimum. It was amazing how they could twist the most innocent thing a person said.

Heather was already at a table and waved. She walked to the waterside table as Heather slid a cup of coffee in front of the extra seat.

"Sorry, I'm late. Had to take the back walkway."

Heather laughed. "I did too. Avoiding Jackie and Jillian."

"Exactly." She rolled her eyes as she sank into the chair beside Heather.

"They caught me when I was leaving the other day. Made remarks on how Father and I were abandoning my—what did they call her—oh—*poor mother*."

"As if your mother couldn't take care of herself."

"Right?" Heather nodded, then frowned. "So... what is it you want to talk about?"

"How did you know I wanted to talk about something?"

"You've got that look."

"You know me too well." She set down her cup. "I have some news. Something I want to talk over with you. You know the cafe next to Parker's?"

"Of course."

"Well... the owner is selling the building. He and his wife are moving out of town. Something about moving near their grandkids." She paused and gathered her thoughts. "And I was thinking... I was going to suggest..."

"Spill it."

"I was thinking we could expand Parker's into that building. Then there would be lots of room to expand the malt shop into more of a gathering area. A coffee bar for the morning crowd. More tables. And that would also give us lots of room in the back of the building, behind the kitchen, to expand Parker's General Store area. Mom is always saying there's more she wants to carry, but there's no more space for it. You know how we have everything so crammed in there. Imagine if we could spread out more and make it look... I don't know... nicer? You know, more like an old-fashioned general store. I think that would attract tourists. Plus, their whole second floor could be used for storage and free more downstairs space for us."

"I think that sounds like a smart business decision."

"I've run some numbers. I don't think it would take long for us to make it a profitable venture. Even with the cost of opening up and connecting the two buildings."

"You have been busy contemplating this, haven't you?"

"I have... and... I'd want to run that part of Parker's. Decide what gets added to the store there. And run the eatery part. The cafe part? I don't know what we'd call it. I was thinking we could offer some things to eat, based on Grandmother's recipes. And her pies, cookies, breads. There's the whole kitchen there."

"Oh, that's a great idea."

"I know it sounds kind of crazy, but that's what I want to do."

"Then you should do it. Put that business learning of yours to work."

"There's the financing of it to consider. I'm not sure if Mom would be on board on taking out a loan against Parker's to do it."

Heather leaned forward. "Not a problem. How about if I help you out? How about I invest in it?"

"You? I mean, it will cost a lot. I can show you the numbers."

"I..." Heather shrugged. "I have the money.

Let's just say my business is doing... ah... well, it's doing *well*."

"How *well*?" She eyed her cousin. They rarely spoke money.

"Well enough to buy the building and give you some start-up money for the rehab."

"Seriously?"

Heather grinned. "Seriously."

"I'm not surprised. You're so talented. I just didn't know." Why hadn't her cousin ever let on how well she was doing, even to her?

"And I think it sounds like a good investment. I can't imagine wanting to invest in anything more than something that will give you your chance to shine."

"You'll have to look at my numbers. See my plans."

"I will. But I trust you. If you think this will work... then let's do it."

Her mind raced with the possibilities. The chance to make this something of her own. Expand Parker's. Make her mark. Then she frowned.

"What's wrong?" Heather asked.

"I still have to run all this past Mom. She'd have to agree to combining and connecting the buildings."

"She will."

"I hope so..."

"Finish your coffee. Show me the numbers. Then we're going to go talk to Aunt Donna."

She pulled her tablet out of her purse and pulled up the spreadsheets she'd made. She and Heather pored over the numbers with Heather asking smart questions and offering a few ideas of her own.

"This is going to be great working with you, Heather. Do you think you can stay around for a while and help get this going? Please?"

"I probably could." Heather nodded.

She'd *finally* found a way to persuade Heather to stay around Moonbeam longer. Her idea was looking better and better. Well, except for getting her mother to agree to it...

Donna looked up to see Olivia and Heather headed over to where she was busy restocking various cleaning supplies along the back wall, cramming them into the tiny space they'd allocated to cleaning. They needed more light back here, too. She'd put that on her ever-growing wish list.

"Morning, girls."

"Aunt Donna, we... Livy... has something she wants to discuss with you." Heather stood with her hands on her hips.

Olivia rolled her eyes at her cousin. "Yeah, Mom. Could we maybe step into the office?"

"Sure." She frowned, wondering what in the world Olivia was so serious about. She brushed her hands on her jeans and led the way to her tiny, cramped office. She grabbed a stack of papers off a side chair and motioned for one of the girls to take it. There wasn't room in here for another chair.

Heather sat down and nodded at Olivia. Olivia who looked... nervous?

"So... Mom. I have this idea."

Donna slid into the chair behind the desk and waited for Olivia to continue. At least it didn't sound like this was some kind of problem with Emily. Though, the whole "I need to talk to you" serious face of Olivia's did remind her slightly of all those years ago when Olivia had gotten up the courage to tell her she was pregnant with Emily and had no plans to marry Brett.

"Did you hear that they're selling the building next door?"

"I did. The Redmonds haven't had their heart in running that cafe ever since their daughter moved away. I heard they were moving to Jacksonville to be near her and their grandchildren."

"Right." Olivia nodded. "And I was thinking that presented us with an opportunity."

"What kind of opportunity?"

"Well... we could buy the building. Expand Parker's like you're always saying you wish you had more space. And also, we could expand the malt shop area into more of a cafe or eatery. I don't know what to call it. But have a coffee shop, maybe bakery things. Who knows, maybe sandwiches or something? Just something to get more people here. And then we'd have the extra space in the back of the building to expand Parker's."

Donna's mind reeled at the words rushing at her.

Olivia continued. "And that extra space is something you've been wanting. You said there's more you'd like to carry at Parker's if only we had the space."

"Olivia... I don't know what to say. I'm so busy now just keeping Parker's going. How would I find the time to do all that? And then there's the money..." Donna hated to crush Olivia's idea, but really? Could her daughter not see how swamped she was just keeping Parker's afloat?

"I've found financing for it and I'd take over, be in charge of all the renovations to connect the buildings and the expansion. You wouldn't have to do a thing."

She frowned. "Where did you find financing?"

Heather raised her hand and shrugged. "Me."

"You?"

"Yes, it appears my cousin is more famous-er than she's let on. And she wants to invest in this."

"I want to invest in *Livy*. Let her... let her have her chance."

Donna didn't miss the direct look that Heather gave her. She glanced over at Olivia and saw the excitement that lit up her daughter's face. She hadn't seen her this animated about something in a long time.

She, herself, wasn't much of a risk-taker. At all. The risks she had taken in life seemed to have a way of crushing her. But how could she let her own insecurities and doubts smash her daughter's dreams?

"I've run the numbers, Mom. Talked to an accountant. I ran it past my business professor."

"You have?"

"Of course. I couldn't just jump into suggesting this if I didn't think it would turn a profit."

"I see."

"But, you'd have to agree, of course. Because we'd have to take out some of the wall. I already talked to a contractor about how we could connect the buildings. They're only about three feet apart. We'd have to work with the town to get it approved, but they've approved it before for businesses that have expanded to the building next to them. The contractor didn't think it would be a problem."

"You've thought of everything, haven't you?"

"Probably not." Olivia shook her head. "But I'm trying to cover as many bases as possible before actually doing this. And, of course, the Redmonds would have to take my offer for the building. I've come up with what I believe is a fair price."

She leaned back in her chair, the air sucked

right from her lungs. This was not what she'd expected today. Or any day. Her days were the same and she liked that. This would change things. Change things a lot. She'd be the first to admit she *hated* change.

"Aunt Donna, what do you think?" Heather leaned forward in her chair, pinning her with a hard stare.

"I think…" What did she think? She wanted to say no. Say it's just too much. Say Parker's was fine the way it was. She looked over as Olivia shifted from foot to foot, waiting for an answer.

"I think if you can make it work and have the financing, then… I'm okay with it." She forced a smile. "I'm *fine* with it." Did that sound convincing? "I think it sounds… promising."

Olivia rushed around the desk and hugged her. "Oh, Mom. You won't regret this, I promise. It's going to be awesome. Just awesome."

Awesome. She sure hoped so. For her own sake and more importantly, for Olivia's. She didn't want to see Olivia's dreams get crushed.

Donna worked the rest of the afternoon kind of on autopilot. Pointing out where the paint was. Helping someone find a cleaner for a hardwood floor. Okaying Melody Tanner to run up yet more on her tab here at Parker's. She really should deal with that, but so far she hadn't had the heart to insist Melody pay off part of her growing bill. Her husband had died last year and Melody seemed to be just scrambling to keep her feet under her as a young widow.

She turned at the sound of yet another customer entering Parker's and self-consciously tucked back a lock of hair when she saw it was Barry. He waved and came over to where she was stocking the latest phone chargers. It was surprising how many tourists came to town and forgot their chargers.

"There you are." He gave her a warm smile. A smile that reached from his lips to clear, sky blue eyes.

The fact he had such sky blue eyes startled her. The fact that she hadn't noticed this before now startled her even more. How had she not noticed their color before this?

"Hi," she replied as she scanned her gaze over him. Or the fact that his brown hair had just a thread or two of gray in it. And the fact he was in need of a haircut. Just a bit of one. She realized she was staring and quickly turned to hang up another charger.

"You look busy."

"A bit." She turned back to him, careful not to stare this time. "Did you come for more ice cream?"

"I did. Do you have time to join me?"

The store was fairly empty. Lydia, one of their regular workers, was running the cash register. And if she joined him, she could give Olivia a break from the malt shop counter. "Sure, let's grab some ice cream."

They walked over to the counter where Olivia had a pad of paper and was scribbling notes. "Olivia, why don't you take a break? I'll run the counter while I have ice cream with Barry."

Olivia eyed her, then Barry, and a quick smile crossed her face. "Perfect. I need to make a couple calls. I'll use the office. Be back in about fifteen minutes."

"Take your time." She went behind the counter as Olivia slid past. "So, what kind of ice cream today?" She stood across from Barry.

"I think I'll try your mint chocolate chip. Two scoops in a cone."

She nodded. "Great choice." She made his cone and got a scoop of vanilla in a bowl for herself, then sat down next to him.

"So, there's another reason I came by today." Barry took a bit of his ice cream and looked at her with those just-discovered sky blue eyes.

"What's that?"

"I wanted to..." He paused and glanced at his ice cream before turning back at her. "I wondered if..."

She waited for him to continue, her spoonful of ice cream halfway to her lips.

"Would you like to go to dinner with me on The Destiny? I mean... like a date with me?"

"I... uh... when?" *Smooth, really, smooth.*

"This weekend? Is Friday or Saturday good for you?"

"Yes."

He grinned. "Which one?"

"Oh, I think Friday would work better."

"Perfect. I'll make reservations for us."

She nodded and they turned their talk to the weather and restoration on the hotel without another mention of their date. He finished his ice cream and rose. "Thanks for joining me. I should get back to work."

She nodded.

"I'll see you Friday? It leaves at six. Do you want to walk over together? If so, I'll come to your house at five-thirty."

"That sounds good." She nodded yet again.

He walked away and she stared down at her empty ice cream bowl, debating getting another scoop. It wasn't every day someone asked her out on a date.

A date. She was going on a date.

"Mom?" Olivia walked up and slipped behind the counter. "You okay?"

"What?" She gathered her bowl, spoon, and napkin and stood. "Of course."

"You look... funny."

She glanced over toward the door. "Well... it appears your mother is going on a date on Friday."

Olivia grinned. "That's some good news. Now will you please, *please* let me take you shopping?"

She remembered her closet that held the old dated clothes and her indecision on what to wear when Barry had simply come over to grill burgers. She smiled at Olivia. "I think that might be a good idea."

CHAPTER 11

L ater that week Donna went shopping with Olivia and Heather. They dragged her to their favorite shop on Magnolia Avenue, Barbara's Boutique. Margaret, the owner, met them as they came in. It always tickled Donna to think that Barbara's Boutique hadn't been owned by a Barbara in over fifty years... but the original name survived. Though, now that she thought of it... there wasn't a person with the last name Parker running Parker's General Store, either. But at least she was a Parker descendant.

She shook her thoughts away and back to the problem at hand. Clothes shopping.

"Donna, I haven't seen you in here in a

while." Margaret frowned. "Actually, I can't remember the last time you've been in here."

Olivia laughed. "I'm sure the last time she was here was probably to buy a present for me. Mom just doesn't go shopping for herself. But she needs an outfit. For a dinner date on The Destiny."

"A date?" Margaret's eyes widened. "Well, I'm sure we can find something perfect."

"I don't want anything fancy."

"Do you want to wear a dress or maybe slacks and a top?" Heather asked.

"I... well, I don't know." Donna looked at the racks of clothes surrounding her, starting to panic just a bit. So many choices.

"Okay, let's say a casual dress." Olivia sifted through some dresses on the rack before her. She picked out two and held them up. "Like either of these?"

"I guess so?" She wasn't sure.

"You like yellow, so try that one on for sure." Heather pointed to the simple yellow dress with elbow-length sleeves.

"I like this black one, though, too, and you could brighten it up with a scarf or a wrap." Olivia raised the other dress. "Try them both on."

Margaret put the dresses in a dressing room and Donna entered. She slipped off her usual worn slacks and Parker's t-shirt—she was heading right back to work when they were finished shopping, after all. She put on the yellow dress and turned this way and that, looking at her reflection in the mirror. The dress *was* pretty. It was fitted at the top but swung loosely around her legs and hit about knee length. The material was a soft jersey and draped nicely from her waist. She opened the door to the dressing room and stepped out.

"Oh, Mom. That looks great on you." Olivia clapped her hands. "Just great."

"But try on the other one to be sure," Heather added.

Donna went back in and switched into the black dress. She barely recognized herself in the mirror. The dress gave her a bit of a sophisticated look. Dressier than the yellow one, by far. But it fit her like it was made for her. She walked out to show the girls.

"Wow." Heather stood there staring at her. "That's just... wow."

"You look fabulous, Mom."

"Don't you think it's way too fancy for The

Destiny?" She frowned as she ran her hands down the sides of the dress.

Olivia puckered her lips. "Maybe. But it sure looks great on you."

"Why don't you get them both? Then, if he asks you out again—hopefully, to somewhere fancier—you'll have the black dress to wear," Heather suggested.

Donna laughed. "I haven't even gone out with him this first time. I don't think I should be planning on a second date quite yet."

Olivia handed her an armful of clothes. "While we have you here, I picked out some more outfits for you. Slacks, sweaters, tops. Try some more on. Your wardrobe could use some —how can I put this nicely—freshening up."

"I don't know..."

"Come on, Aunt Donna. It will be fun."

Donna went back in and put on one of the outfits Olivia had picked out for her. Simple black pants—that weren't worn out or faded to a dusky gray like the few pairs she had at home—and a short-sleeved white sweater top with a bit of black trim. The girls approved of that outfit along with a knit skirt and striped top and a casual sleeveless dress. They vetoed a loud floral sundress, then approved of a pair of navy slacks and red top.

She got dressed back into her now decidedly old and worn clothes and went out to join the girls. As she walked out of the dressing room and saw the stack of clothing, she almost gasped. "I can't buy all of that."

"Of course you can. Who knows how many years it will be before I can get you back in here," Olivia insisted. "Oh, and I found these two scarfs. They'll go great with a couple of the outfits. So, you're all set."

Margaret rang everything up and Donna looked at the bags of clothes, feeling guilty. Like really guilty. It seemed like such a splurge. But they really weren't that expensive. Margaret carried reasonably priced lines of clothing. But still, it was a lot of new clothes all at once.

Olivia gathered up the bags, handing some to Heather. "Now, we're going next door to the shoe store."

"Wait. No, I've gotten enough new things."

"Mom, you can't wear your work shoes with these. Look at them." Olivia pointed at her sensible, if worn, black shoes. "We'll find you some simple black flats and maybe another dressier pair of shoes."

Thirty minutes later Donna walked out of the shoe store with three new pairs of shoes. The simple black flats, a low-heeled sandal, and a pair of bright red slip-on wedges. She stood on the sidewalk, a bit in shock.

Heather hugged her and laughed. "It will all be okay, Aunt Donna. Your closet may have a bit of shock when you put all this in there, but everyone should get new clothes every now and again."

"And, Mom, you haven't gotten anything new in years." Olivia dumped the packages in her car that was parked in front of them on the street. "I'm going to run all these home for you, then I'll meet you at Parker's."

"You don't have to do that."

"I'm going to take them to your house, cut off the tags, and hang them up. I want to make sure you don't return them all when Heather and I aren't there to watch over you." Olivia grinned as she got into her car.

Donna said goodbye and walked down the sidewalk to Parker's. She had to admit she'd loved the new outfits. She looked down at her worn slacks and Parker's t-shirt. Maybe she should consider getting a few more outfits for work that didn't look so old and tired...

That would have to wait. She'd had enough of a clothing shock for one day. A smile played at the corners of her mouth while she hummed a song and hurried back to Parker's to get to work.

Donna looked up to see Delbert enter Parker's with a woman hanging possessively on his arm. Maybe the Camille he'd mention at The Cabot?

The woman frowned just inside the door. "Really? Here?" she exclaimed in an incredulous tone.

Donna walked up to them and smiled.

"Welcome, Del. What brings you to Parker's today?"

"Been craving your ice cream, of course." He winked, then turned to the woman beside him—the woman with the frown plastered on her perfectly made-up face with her perfectly put together trendy outfit. "Camille, this is Donna. She owns the general store."

Camille looked her over carefully, her gaze running from the top of her disheveled curls, to her faded work clothes, to the tired, worn-out work shoes. "Pleased to meet you," she said without any warmth.

"Nice to meet you." Donna plastered on a welcoming smile. She knew how to deal with difficult customers. Years of training.

"I wanted Camille to try some of your delicious ice cream."

"I don't suppose you have sugar free?" Camille cocked her head to the side.

"Ah... no, we don't."

"Well, I guess I could have one scoop in a dish." Camille's forehead creased. "But, Delbert, why you'd take me to a *general store* to get food is... well, *strange*, at best."

"Best ice cream I've ever had." Delbert led Camille over to the malt counter and Donna trailed along, hoping to provide some moral support if Camille said something not so nice to Olivia.

"Good afternoon, Del. How are you today?" Olivia greeted them with a wide smile.

"Olivia, this is Camille."

"Hey, Camille, great to meet you. Any friend of Del's and all that." Another wide smile.

Camille barely nodded at Olivia in acknowledgment. "So, where do we sit?" She looked around at the handful of small cafe tables like they were dirty or totally unacceptable.

"Right here at the counter." Del climbed onto a stool.

"At the counter?"

"Best place to eat it." Delbert nodded.

Camille let out a long sigh, grabbed a napkin to wipe off the already sparkling clean seat, and slowly climbed onto it, perched carefully at the very edge.

"I'm in for butter pecan today. Two scoops in a cone." Del smiled at Olivia.

"I guess I'll just have vanilla. In a dish. No cone." Camille let out yet another sigh.

"Best vanilla ever," Olivia said as she went to make their orders.

Camille's eyebrows rose in frank disbelief.

"What brings you to town, Camille?" Donna asked in her friendliest tone. Well, as friendly as she could manage. She was still bristling at Camille's weak acknowledgment when she was introduced to Olivia.

"Delbert wanted me to see The Cabot. The renovations."

"Oh, it's gorgeous, isn't it?" Olivia said as she gave them their ice cream.

Camille frowned yet again. "Gorgeous? *I*

think it looks... outdated. And it was dusty from construction and so noisy."

"I think it looks... vintage and elegant, and I just love what Del has done with it," Olivia said.

"I guess. If you like that type of thing. I much prefer the more classic Hamilton Hotels."

A customer needed her attention and Donna reluctantly turned to help them and left Olivia to fend for herself. When she finally made it back to the counter, Del and Camille were just getting ready to leave and she recognized the fake smile on Olivia's face and the tight set of her mouth.

She forced a cheerful tone. "So, did you enjoy the ice cream?"

"As always," Delbert affirmed.

"It was just *ice cream*." Camille shrugged as she turned and swept her gaze around the shop. "The store is so... *worn*, I guess. Don't you ever update it and make it more modern? And how does one ever find something in here?"

"There's always someone to help a customer if they can't find something."

Camille looked doubtful. "Well... this was an... interesting trip to Moonbeam, but I'm ready to get back to Belle Island. Delbert, are you ready to leave?"

Del nodded, then turned to Olivia. "Thanks for the ice cream. Delicious as usual. See you soon."

His tone was almost apologetic as if compensating for Camille's rude remarks.

Camille kept a wide berth from any of the displays as they were leaving, then she paused for Del to open the door for her. They slipped outside and Donna turned to Olivia. "Camille is... something."

"Right, and I'm not allowed to use the words to describe what kind of something I think she is." Olivia grinned. "I wonder what Del sees in her?"

"I'm not sure. He seems so down to earth and a genuinely kind person. And she is... well..."

"Full of herself?"

Donna laughed. "Yes, that's one way to put it." She turned to get back to work as more customers came in the door.

CHAPTER 12

"Mom, you look beautiful."

Donna walked out into the bedroom in her new yellow dress and black flats.

"How about you let me do your makeup?" Olivia's eyes lit up.

"I don't usually wear much makeup." Donna frowned.

"You don't. And I won't overdo it. I promise. Come here. Sit by the window and let me fix your makeup and hair."

"My hair?"

"I'm going to put it up so it doesn't bother you in the wind on the boat, but will look nice and..."

"And not wild?" She let out a gentle laugh.

"That." Olivia spread out a bag of makeup on the dresser beside them.

Soon Olivia had applied eye makeup, a bit of foundation and blush, and a nice subtle lipstick. Then she piled up her curls and twisted them into a knot, with a few tresses drifting around her face.

"There. Look in the mirror." Olivia stood back to look at her handiwork.

Donna got up and walked over to the mirror. She stared at her reflection. "I can't... I mean... that doesn't even look like me."

"Of course it does, Mom. You're beautiful." Olivia hugged her.

She touched the soft fabric of the dress and reached up toward her hair, but didn't mess with it. It was too lovely to touch. Olivia had kept her word, and the makeup was subtle but highlighted her hazel eyes and gave a bit of color to her high cheekbones.

"You did a great job, hon."

The doorbell rang and she quickly looked in the mirror again, gulping a big breath of air. Her pulse raced through her veins. A date. She was going on a date.

Olivia hurried off to answer the door. "Hey, Barry. Mom will be out in a minute."

Donna peeked into the front room and saw Barry standing there with nice dress pants and a collared knit shirt. As she entered the room, his eyes grew wide.

"Wow, you look smashing."

Her cheeks flushed.

"She does look great when we get her out of her Parker clothes, doesn't she? Not that she doesn't look great at work, too." Olivia grinned. "But I did have fun helping her get ready."

"Yes, she does look great all the time." Barry stumbled over his words.

Olivia laughed. "You two have a good time. See you later." With that, she slipped out the door.

The front room was deafeningly silent with Olivia gone. She stood there, not knowing what to say.

"Ah, well, we should go. Don't want to be late. I doubt they'll hold the boat for us." Barry opened the door and she slipped through.

So very close to him as she passed. Close enough to smell a woodsy aftershave on his freshly shaven face. And somewhere along the way, he'd gotten a haircut, and his brown hair lay precisely in a proper businessman cut. He stepped out and she turned to lock the door, bumping into him as she turned.

"Oh, sorry." Those sky blue eyes that she'd discovered lit up with his smile.

She ignored her thumping heart, concentrated on the lock, and then took a step back. "Okay. All set."

They headed down the sidewalk toward the marina. She watched each step she took in her pretty new black flats. The awkward silence clung to them as they strolled down the street.

Talk to her. Think of something. Anything. Silence again. Why did he keep suddenly forgetting how to speak around her? Barry searched his mind for a topic of conversation.

"I wonder what kind of food they'll have on the dinner cruise." Though he knew darn well —he'd looked it up on their website. But it seemed like a safe subject and the first thing that popped into his mind.

"I'm not sure. I haven't been on it since Jesse took it over."

Well, he'd messed that one up. Now he

couldn't tell her that there was a seafood buffet because he'd claimed lack of knowledge.

Suddenly he stopped and touched her elbow. She paused beside him.

"Look, I don't know why, but I'm ridiculously nervous. And I can't think of what to say. And I do know what The Destiny has tonight. It's a seafood buffet. I was just looking for something to start a conversation with. I'm sorry. I'm just not very good at this dating thing." He spit it all out as though it were one sentence.

Donna let out a long breath of air. "Oh, good."

"What's good?" His forehead wrinkled.

"You're as nervous as I am. I was going to start talking about the weather because, you know... safe." She laughed, and it spread all the way to her sparkling hazel eyes.

The laughter cut the tension between them, and they continued on their way to the marina in an easy conversation like on their previous walks. Relief washed through him knowing that Donna was nervous, too. They'd just figure the night out together.

They got to the boat and were greeted on

the gangway by a young man with blonde hair and steel blue eyes.

"Jesse, it's good to see you." Donna hugged the man.

"Donna, glad you could make it on The Destiny."

"I should have made time earlier. I've only heard wonderful things about it since you took it over."

"Thanks." Jesse beamed.

"Oh, this is Barry. He's coordinating the rehab of The Cabot Hotel."

Jesse held out his hand and shook Barry's. "Great to meet you. Can't wait to have the hotel up and running again. I've missed her. And welcome aboard. Why don't you grab a drink, then go up to the open upper deck? Great view up there."

They each got a glass of wine, then took the spiral staircase to the upper level. He trailed behind Donna as they spiraled up between the decks. They got to the wide, open upper level. Benches and seats lined the railings.

"There are some open seats." He pointed.

They took two seats to watch The Destiny pull away from the dock and enter the bay. The further they got into the bay, the clearer the water was that circled around them.

"The water near the marina is a bit brackish with the river dumping fresh water into the bay. As we get closer to the gulf, the water clears up into this fabulous turquoise color," Donna explained.

The wind picked up as they cruised along. Donna tugged a wrap around her shoulders.

"Are you cold? We could go down inside out of the wind."

Though, he liked the way the wind would pick up little bits of her hair and toss them around her face in delicate curls. Her cheeks were blushed a delicate rose color, and the evening light caught the highlights of her eyes.

"No, I'm fine up here. Glad I grabbed this wrap." She smiled. "Olivia loaned it to me. She's not very impressed with my closet."

"You look beautiful." The words came out before he could even think or catch them back.

She blushed a deeper shade of rose. "Oh, thank you. Olivia took me shopping for this new dress. Did my hair. She tried to transform me from a Parker's worker to ..." Donna shrugged. "To, I'm not sure what."

"Well, you look lovely tonight. And I'm glad

you said yes. It's fun to do things in a new town. Explore a bit." He tilted his head. "Although I guess this isn't really exploring for you."

"It's all new on the boat since Jesse bought it. It's much nicer. New seats. Everything painted this crisp, clean gray color." She smiled up at him. "Anyway, I don't get away from the store often."

"You always seem busy there."

"We are. And..." She paused, her forehead creased with wrinkles. "Olivia came up with this idea that we should expand. It's some dream of hers. Something she can do that will be all hers. Things are a bit hectic now. She's finalizing plans. Has an offer in to buy the building next to Parker's."

"Really?"

"Yes..." The wrinkles stayed creased between her eyes. "But I'm afraid it's going to be so much more work. She assures me she'll handle it all."

"But?" He could hear the hesitation in her voice.

"But what if it fails? What if we can't recoup the cost of expanding? What if her dream gets crushed? I'd hate that."

"What if she gets her dream?" He touched

her hand. "Everyone needs a chance to follow their dreams."

"I know. And I want it to work out for her. I'm just a bit..."

"Afraid?" he asked gently. He could see it plainly on her face.

"Yes. I am afraid. I'm not a risk-taker and this seems like a big risk."

"And yet you said yes and you're letting her do it." She'd said yes because Olivia was her daughter and they had strong family ties. He admitted to a twinge of jealousy. What would it be like to have family ties like that?

"I am. How could I say no? How could I not give her a chance?"

"I could look at her plans if you'd like. Maybe make some suggestions. If it wouldn't hurt her feelings. I'm pretty good at this rehab stuff, you know." He grinned.

"So I've heard." Donna smiled. "I'll talk to her. See if she'd like you to look over the plans. It would make me feel better if you don't think her whole plan is impossible."

"I'd be more than happy to. Just let me know."

An announcement came on that the buffet was open, and most of the people on the upper level headed back downstairs to the large eating area. "Want to go?" he asked.

"If you're not too hungry, I'm just enjoying the view and drinking our wine."

"Suits me just fine."

Yes, he was perfectly fine sitting here right next to this fascinating woman.

They sat outside as the sun played hide and seek with the clouds and the sky started to burst into colors. Seagulls swooped overhead in the evening light. Barry sat right beside her, inches from her. His leg brushing hers through her new dress everyone once in a while when he turned to look at something, his hair mussed from the breeze. His eyes sparkling in the evening light.

She was surprised at how much she was enjoying herself. How relaxing it was... in a kind of underlying tension kind of way. But that was just a bit of her nerves still talking.

Her nerves. Like when she'd told him about her pathetic closet and Olivia basically dressing her for this date. Did he think she didn't know how to dress herself? Or that she thought this date was some kind of really big deal? It wasn't.

It was simply a night out with a man whose company she enjoyed. Enjoyed quite a bit, actually.

She turned to sneak a peek at him and found him staring at her.

"Sorry. I just wondering what you were thinking," he said. "You looked lost in thought."

"I was just thinking what a pleasant night it is. The view is wonderful." Safe topics. Stay on safe topics.

"It is." But he didn't take his eyes off her when he said it.

Warmth rushed to her cheeks. "Well, we should probably go eat." She stood quickly.

"As you wish." He rose beside her and led the way to the spiral staircase down to the main room.

They filled their plates with a delicious looking variety of seafood and found a table by the window that had just been vacated. More people headed back upstairs and the crowd in the dining area thinned. Barry snagged them both another glass of wine and sat across from her.

He regaled her with stories of mishaps on the remodel at the hotel. "But I think I'm getting things turned around. Fixed some orders for supplies we need. Had them repaint the library room that we're using for the history alcove. Someone got it in their minds that it was supposed to be orange…" He chuckled in deep, resonant tones. "That got changed. I thought Emily was going to faint when she came in and saw it painted orange this week. I don't know who messed up the paint colors, but I didn't catch it until they'd painted half the room. It's a nice, soft, pale shade of green now, and Emily heartily approves."

"She told me she's been in there twice this week. Having such a grand time sorting through all the memorabilia."

"Del has her boxing up any old accounting records that she comes across. He's not ready to pitch those yet. She found the original handwritten register from when the hotel was first opened. She was thrilled with that find. And she found some old furniture in storage that we're going to use to display some of the keepsakes that she finds. The furniture cases are a deep mahogany wood with the original glass in them. Quite a find."

"I'm sure she's thrilled with her new job."

"But I guess it's not a great time to leave you

short-handed, is it? What with Olivia's plans for expansion."

"We'll get along. Emily does love her history."

"She sure seems too. Her eyes light up when she brings me some new thing that she's found. Very enthusiastic."

"That she is. She's a bit of a whirlwind at all times. Hard worker. And..." Donna grinned. "As you can tell I'm an unbiased grandmother."

"Totally unbiased, I can tell." His eyes twinkled as the corners of his mouth twitched in a smile.

They finished dinner and headed back up top as the boat headed back toward the dock. They stood along the railing, watching the water slip past. She shivered slightly and pulled her wrap tighter around her shoulders.

"You're cold."

"A bit."

He stood behind her and wrapped his arms around her, pulling her close. "That better?"

"Uh-huh." She managed to get that much out. It was better than better. It was... very nice. It was very pleasant standing wrapped in his arms. Her pulse picked up and she ignored it because, after all, he was just keeping her warm in the night breeze.

All too soon the boat docked and everyone slowly filed off the boat. Jesse thanked them for coming. "Come back soon."

"I will. And I'll tell the girls to come soon. They'll love it. You've really made it lovely, Jesse."

"Thanks, Donna. Means a lot to me. Always been a dream of mine, and when she came up for sale, I jumped on it."

"You made the right decision. The Destiny is wonderful."

She and Barry headed down the gangway and onto the long dock. They slowly strolled along until they got to the wharf, then turned to head back to their houses. He kept one arm around her shoulders as they walked. Probably to keep her warm still. Though, it wasn't as chilly now that they were off the boat and out of the breeze. It was actually rather pleasant out. Not that she was going to turn down his arm around her.

They got to Sandpiper Court way too quickly as far as she was concerned. He walked her to her doorstep and they stood there in the darkness, the night air heavy around them.

"Thank you. I had a really nice time." She dug for her key and unlocked the door.

"I had a great time, too, Donna." His voice was low and he stood so close to her.

She could feel the electricity between them. A magnetic pull. A... something.

And just like that she panicked and swung the door open. "Thanks again." She flipped on the inside light and light spilled out onto the porch. "Good night."

A disappointed looked flitted across his face, but then he smiled. "Good night, Donna."

She went inside, closed the door behind her, and leaned against it, her heart pounding. She'd been so sure he was getting ready to kiss her. He was, wasn't he? And the whole is he or isn't he question just put her in a tizzy. She was one silly woman, she chastised herself.

She pushed off the door and walked further inside, sorry she hadn't just let him kiss her. *If* that was what he'd been about to do...

CHAPTER 13

"Mom. Mom!" Olivia's voice rang through the house.

Donna looked up from the sink where she was washing dishes. She grabbed a towel to dry her hands. "In the kitchen."

Olivia rushed into the room. "I got it. The Redmonds said my offer was fair. I've got the building." She whirled around in a close imitation of Emily's antics. "I can't believe it. It's going to be so great. And I have plans to spruce up all of Parker's after we get more space. Make it more like it was before when I was little. Before we loaded it up with so much stuff. Like an old-fashioned general store... only... well, with things people need now."

"One step at a time."

"It's all part of the plan. Once it's all done, it will be wonderful. Just you wait and see. You'll love it."

Donna paused, wondering if she should ask or not. She didn't want to offend her daughter or make her think she didn't trust her business decisions. She decided to take the plunge. "So, Barry said he'd look over your plans if you'd like. He does have a lot of expertise in remodeling businesses."

Olivia stopped and stood still, staring hard at her. "Are you having doubts?"

"No, of course not. I just thought you might like some help. Or he could offer suggestions. Or..." She could see the troubled look on Olivia's face. "Or not. If you'd rather not."

Olivia stepped forward. "No, that sounds like a good idea. And if he looks at them and approves... will you feel better about all of this?"

"It's not that I don't feel good about this..."

"Mom, I know. It's a lot of change. You hate change."

"I don't hate change." But she did.

"I promise, it's going to be great. And I'll accept any help he gives. I want this to be a success, and if he can make it better, or more cost-effective, I'm all ears."

"Good."

"I'll drop by The Cabot Hotel and talk to him. See if I can email him my business plan and some spreadsheets." Olivia gave her a quick hug. "Mom, it's all going to be fine. You'll see."

Her daughter turned around and hurried back out, the door closing with a dull thud as she left.

Now all she had to worry about is if Barry looked at the plans and thought they were in over their heads. Because, to tell the truth, that's the way she was feeling.

She looked at her watch. If she didn't hurry she was going to be late meeting Evelyn at the wharf. Her sister had called and invited her to dinner at Portside Grill again. She really preferred Jimmy's, but Evelyn wasn't a big fan of their casual style. Her sister had sounded a bit lonely, so she'd agreed to meet her again. When was that husband of hers going to come home? When Darren was in town, she rarely saw Evelyn while they wined and dined his business associates and partied at the country club.

She had just enough time to slip on the navy

pants and red top that she'd gotten when she went shopping with Olivia and Heather. She could even grudgingly admit Olivia had been right. It was nice to have some new clothing options to wear.

Evelyn was waiting at a table for Donna when she got to Portside Grill. She joined her sister and smiled as a waiter came up with two glasses of white wine.

"I ordered us pinot grigio, hope that's okay."

"Yes, that's perfect."

"Here are your menus, and the special tonight is a basil and lemon ricotta stuffed salmon served with asparagus with a lemon sauce. It's very good. I'll be back soon to get your orders."

He left them alone, and Donna took a sip of her wine. "Oh, that's good."

"They have an excellent wine list here. I'm glad. There's a lack of good wine lists in this town."

And there was something that would never even hit Donna's consciousness. The quality of wine lists in Moonbeam. She and her sister had always been so very different.

Evelyn looked at her carefully. "Is that a new outfit?"

"Yes, Olivia and Heather took me shopping."

"Heather went?"

Ah, that might have been a mistake to mention. "Yes, Olivia dragged her along. I got a few new things." Her sister didn't have to know just how *many* new things.

"So, for your date with Barry?"

"How did you—never mind. Nothing is secret here. Not that I was keeping it a secret."

"I ran into Jackie and Jillian. They told me."

Of course, they did. "Yes, we went on The Destiny. Jesse's done a great job with that."

"He has?" Evelyn's eyes flew open in surprise.

Donna remembered that Evelyn wasn't much of a fan of Jesse's. He and Heather had been friends growing up and Evelyn and Darren had thought that Jesse wasn't a good influence on Heather. But Donna had always thought he was a fine young man. Just one more thing they disagreed on.

"Yes, it was nice. You should go on one of his dinner cruises."

Evelyn looked unconvinced and set her glass down. "So I heard that you bought the building next to Parker's."

Well, that was a ping-pong subject change. "Ah... well, Olivia did. She wants to expand the store."

"And you think it's wise to take out a loan now? Didn't you say that you were just getting Parker's to a profitable spot these days?"

Now what was she supposed to say? Evelyn obviously didn't know about Heather investing in the store. So, she evaded the question. "I think it will work out."

"I don't know how you can even consider it. You're so busy as it is."

"Olivia says she'll be in charge of it all. And she's very excited about it."

She could see the clear disapproval on Evelyn's face. So maybe it wasn't so much that her sister was lonely tonight, but that she wanted to voice her opinion about the expansion of Parker's.

"I still think it's risky." Her sister's voice was edged with disapproval.

"A bit. But we'll make it work. Olivia has

grand plans about sprucing up Parker's and making it look more like the old general store instead of how cramped and cluttered it's become as we added more inventory. I think that will attract more tourists to come in. And if she expands the malt shop into more of an eatery—or cafe or something like that. She's thinking baked goods and maybe even sandwiches."

"But you don't cook. Or bake. Neither does Olivia, does she?"

"No, we'd have to hire someone. Olivia wants to use Grandmother's recipes for a lot of the things she'd offer."

"Really?" Evelyn nodded at that, finally approving of something. "They are the best recipes ever."

Donna knew that Evelyn often made their grandmother's recipes. She was an accomplished pie baker, unlike herself. She could not get a pie crust to taste good or be flakey like Evelyn's no matter what she tried. And she was sure she was using the exact same recipe that Evelyn used. She sighed and took a sip of her wine.

The waiter came and took their order, giving her a chance to segue into a new subject.

"So, I guess Darren is out of town again?" Had he even come back *in* town? She rarely saw him even when he was in Moonbeam.

"Yes, he's out of town." Evelyn fiddled with her fork, caught herself, and left it alone.

"He's been gone a lot."

"He's busy, what can I say?"

Her sister had a strange marriage. She'd never seen much real affection between Evelyn and Darren, though she had to admit they made a smashing couple when they were all dressed up for their numerous fundraisers and business parties. Some of the beautiful people. They often had their photo in the paper from the various events.

Donna had had her photo in the paper exactly one time. The day she'd officially taken over running Parker's. It was a photo of her and her grandparents in front of the store. And it hadn't been exactly flattering.

She'd had on her usually worn slacks and Parker's t-shirt. The day had been hotter than blazes and she'd been busy working in the store when a reporter for the local paper dropped in to write a brief article on the official change of managers. Though, to be honest, even after her official change to manager, her grandparents had often come in to help during the busy season. Most townsfolk *still* considered it her grandparents' store, and her grandparents had passed away years ago.

They finished their dinner chatting about the great weather they'd been having and a new restaurant Evelyn wanted to try in Sarasota. Sounded like another up and coming trendy place that Evelyn would love and she herself would just... go along to please Evelyn and keep her company.

They paid their bill and walked out of the restaurant and down the long wharf. The twinkle lights strung on the storefronts lent a festive air to the wharf at night. She did like coming here even if she only came when Evelyn or Olivia insisted she get out. She much preferred her quiet nights at home, sitting out on the point.

But her sister thrived on activity and people and conversation. She might as well check that off as just another difference between them. She glanced over at Evelyn as they strolled along. Her clothes had no wrinkles, even after sitting for dinner. Her hair was perfectly in place, still.

Her own hair was furled about in a wild mess of curls from the day's humidity. She hadn't gotten the thick, beautiful straight brown hair her sister had inherited from their mother. Her sister had flawless skin, expertly manicured nails, and always kept a trim figure, unlike her own always-need-to-lose fifteen—okay twenty —pounds she carried with her.

They got to the end of the wharf. "I brought my car tonight. Shall I drive you home?" Evelyn asked.

"No, I think I'll walk. It's so nice out."

"Okay, I guess I'll see you soon." Evelyn turned, walked over to her fancy sports car, and drove away.

Yet another difference. She'd always pick walking to places in Moonbeam if at all possible. Her sister avoided walking around town for more than a block. How could they have come from the same parents? She shrugged and turned to head back to Sandpiper Court. She still had time to sit outside under the stars and maybe have a cup of chamomile tea.

Donna made herself tea, pouring the hot water into a delicate floral teacup that had been part of her grandmother's collection. It always made her feel close to her grandmother when she used one of her teacups. She kicked off her shoes by the back door. Just as she was ready to head outside, she heard a knock at the front door. She glanced at her watch, wondering who would come by at eight-thirty at night. She set down her tea and went to answer the door.

Barry stood there looking impossibly handsome, and she was glad she had on her nice new slacks and top. She self-consciously tugged at the hem of her red top to straighten it.

He smiled. "I hope I'm not too late. I saw your lights come on and knew you just got home. I came over earlier, but there was no answer."

"I was out to eat with Evelyn." She motioned him inside. "Come in. I was just going to have a cup of chamomile tea. Would you like one?"

"I've never had that before. Sure, I'd love to try it."

"I'm using one of my grandmother's teacups, but I could make yours in a mug." She led him into the kitchen and motioned to her cup sitting on the counter.

"Might be safer. I'd hate to break something so delicate."

She made his tea in a mug and they carried their drinks out to the Adirondack chairs on the point and sat down. He turned to her. "So, Olivia came by today and said she'd like for me to look at her business plan and her spreadsheets."

"Oh, good. She said she'd take any suggestions you could give."

"She emailed them to me and I went over them closely. She's done a great job with the plan. I can see from what she's done that she has a good head for business. Her numbers and projections are realistic, I think. She included photos of what she'd like the new cafe area to look like and how she'd make the store part more old-fashioned general store-like."

"She did? I haven't seen those."

"I emailed her back a few minor suggestions and things to look into, but all in all, it's a good, solid plan."

Donna relaxed back against the chair. "That makes me feel better. Not that I doubted her, but it's nice to have her plan confirmed as reasonable and hopefully profitable for us."

"Is she going to run Parker's after you're... well, after you finish managing it? You know, after you retire?"

"I... ah... we've never really talked about it. I assume so." She frowned. Why hadn't she ever talked to Olivia about that? Olivia wanted to stay, didn't she? Or... did she want to go out and do something different?

"I got the impression that this is her way of making her mark on the store, so I assumed she was going to take over eventually." He gazed at her intently.

So, maybe this expansion *was* Olivia's something different.

She could see that more clearly now and promised herself she'd be more enthusiastic and supportive. "I should talk to her about the future of Parker's. You're right. And I appreciate you taking the time to look at the plans."

"It was no problem. Love to help in any way I can." He gave her an easy, friendly smile in the moonlight. "And this tea is good, by the way."

She smiled back at him. "I sometimes come out here and sip chamomile if I can't wind down enough to go to bed."

"And does it help?"

"Either the tea, or the view, or the starlight does... or maybe it's all of it."

They sat and sipped tea and chatted until Barry finally looked at his watch. "Oh, look at that. We've been out here over two hours. I should go." He stood.

She rose beside him, surprised that much time had gone by. He was so easy to talk to and a good listener, too. She'd loved hearing about the details of his day at The Cabot.

They went inside and she put their cups in the sink and walked him through to the front door.

"Thanks for the tea. And the conversation." He tossed her one of his easy smiles.

"It was nice."

He crossed over to his house and paused to wave before he disappeared inside. She slowly closed the door and turned to go wash the dishes in the sink.

What a nice evening she'd had.

Very nice.

She smiled again at the easy, comfortable camaraderie they'd developed between them. Barry Richmond was an interesting man and she very much enjoyed spending time with him.

CHAPTER 14

"Barry, you should see the paintings I found."

Barry looked up to see Emily at his office door the next afternoon, her eyes lit up, holding up a painting in each hand.

"I looked on the back of them and they're all labeled. It's a bunch of Cabots. And a family portrait too. Looks to be maybe three generations of Cabots in one portrait."

He came around the desk to look at them. "Those are great finds. We should definitely put them up in the history alcove."

"I thought so. We could get some nice labels made to hang under them to say who each person is. Maybe a little write-up of when they owned or worked at the hotel."

"That's a great idea. Can you take care of that?"

"Of course." She nodded enthusiastically. "And some workers moved those display cases to the library for me. I have some things set up in there. Not sure where I'll place everything yet, but it's a start."

"Come on, why don't you show me what you've done." They headed to the library and Emily leaned the two paintings against the wall.

"I thought the big family portrait could go over there." She pointed to a blank wall between two large built-in shelving units. "And across from that, on this wall, we could do a series of the other paintings." She twirled around and pointed at one more area. "And there, on that small wall, I thought we could put up a bunch of the old black and white photos I've found of the hotel through the years. I found one from when the hotel first opened before they'd added on any of the additions."

"I like all your ideas. You just let me know if you need something to make it happen."

"This is like my best job ever. For sure." Emily's genuine smile stretched across her face.

"And I like to hear that." Delbert Hamilton

strolled into the library, with Camille holding onto his arm. "Hi, Barry, you remember Camille. And Emily, I'd like you to meet Camille Montgomery."

Camille barely nodded his direction. Okay, then.

"Miss Montgomery, nice to meet you." Emily walked up, the smile still large on her features. "Del, you should see what I've found for the history alcove."

"Del?" Camille peered down her nose at Emily. "You mean Mr. Hamilton?"

"He... he said to call him—" Emily's eyes widened.

"Camille, darlin'. I told her to call me Del. We don't need the formalities here."

Camille didn't look like she approved and thought that all formalities should immediately be reinstated.

"Ah... so... do you want to see what I found?"

"I'm sure *Mr. Hamilton* is too busy to be bothered by all the little details of your job." Camille frowned. "What is your job? You look... young."

"I'm putting together the history alcove here. Sorting through all the historical memorabilia and finding some Cabot family portraits."

Camille turned to Del. "Delbert, seriously, you're not going to have this young girl put together the history alcove are you? I mean, you need to use an interior designer, make sure everything looks... well..." A shadow of disapproval etched her face. "You need to make sure it looks... *professional*. Classic. Refined."

Emily took a step back and stiffened, her hands slowly balling into fists before she jammed them into her pockets. Her cheeks flushed crimson.

"You can't simply hire a child to do that."

Emily struggled to fight back tears. She was so proud of her work here.

Delbert stepped forward. "Emily is doing a fine job. She has lots of knowledge of the town and is a big lover of history. She even works at Moonbeam's History Museum. I can't think of a *better* person for the job." His voice rang out strong and assured.

"If you need to get someone else, I understand. A real designer or something." Emily's voice was low.

Delbert stepped over to Emily and touched her arm. "No, Emily. I won't be doing that.

You're doing a wonderful job and I appreciate all the effort you're putting into it. I couldn't pay someone who didn't have... I don't know... the heart that you're putting into this. I'm pleased with everything you've done. You're in charge. I trust you."

Emily's eyes lit up again. "Thank you, De— Ah, thanks. I won't let you down."

Camille's eyes flashed. "You'll regret this, Delbert, mark my words. Your choices sometimes..." She shook her head, her tone an icy condemnation.

"Hey, Emily, let's go back to the storeroom and you can show me that family portrait you found. I'd love to see it." Barry smiled encouragingly at Emily, wanting to get her away from Camille. He then turned to Camille and nodded briefly toward her. "Camille." And he didn't care one bit how cold his tone sounded, though she probably didn't notice she was so wrapped up in herself. He'd never figure out what Del saw in the woman.

He led Emily out of the library and away from Camille and her hurtful words. A fierce protective streak surged through him toward Donna's granddaughter. She didn't deserve to be spoken to like that and the tears at the corners of her eyes had tugged at his heart. He hadn't been much of a fan of Camille's before, ever since he'd met her at a fancy New Year's Eve party a few years back, and now he certainly wasn't.

Delbert Hamilton turned to Camille and in spite of his best intentions, a long sigh escaped his lips. He paused so he could choose his words carefully. "Camille, darlin', you know I care about you, but I can't have you talking that way to people. You need to learn to think before you speak. You can't go around hurting people's feelings."

"I can speak how I want, Delbert. You shouldn't have this... *girl*... in charge of something like that. That's absurd."

"She's doing a wonderful job. It's a great opportunity for her, and I was happy to give it to her. And... it's my decision to make." He took a step back and rubbed his temple. Dating Camille was often... complicated.

"And why are you taking their side?" Camille stamped her foot, anger flashing across her face, her eyes darkening.

"I'm not taking sides. I'm saying I won't have you disparaging people I care about."

"You don't care about her. She just works for you." Camille looked truly bewildered.

"I care about everyone who works for me. Everyone who works for Hamilton Hotels. They are part of my extended family, and their welfare is important to me."

"That's a silly notion. Of course, they aren't your family."

"They are," he insisted. "And I'd appreciate if you'd treat them as such." He sighed. "Camille, this is important to me. Very important." He knew crossing Camille was a dangerous proposition, but he really did want her to understand how important this was.

"If this silly little girl's feelings are more important than me, then I guess I'll just go back to Belle Island. I can see I'm not wanted here."

He stood, and for what might have been the first time, he truly saw her, the real Camille. She was impeccably dressed. Always was. She carried herself with— there was no other way to describe it—a *haughty* air. She was entertaining and he often enjoyed her company. But she was... So. Much. Work.

She stood there staring at him, waiting for

him to apologize, which was how he usually handled their disagreements. It was just easier to not rile her.

But this time he just slowly nodded. "I think you returning to Belle Island might be for the best."

"Really, you aren't going to apologize and ask me to stay?" Her eyes widened.

"No, I'm not," he said simply.

"Well, don't expect to see me come begging you to take me back. We're over, Delbert Hamilton. Finished. I will not be treated like this." Camille twirled around and stalked across the foyer, her heels clicking on the tile floor with each furious step she took. She paused by the door and turned back to him. "I'll send your driver back for you after he drops me off on Belle Island."

She flounced out the front door and suddenly the entryway was silent.

Very silent.

And he found he didn't mind the silence at all.

He'd tried so hard with Camille, thinking she'd change. Thinking that she'd soften. He realized he was tired of listening to her criticism, her complaints. Oh, she could be charming when she wanted to. Or when she wanted something. But, truth be told, he was getting tired of constantly trying to keep her happy. Relationships took work, but usually, it took work from *both* halves of the couple.

He ran his hand through his hair and tugged his collar loose. The blessed silence still echoed through the entranceway.

He turned and headed off to find Emily to see if he could make amends. He was so very tired of making amends for Camille, too.

Maybe the break was a good thing. He needed a change and time to think.

CHAPTER 15

Donna wasn't certain she'd made the right decision with the whole expansion of Parker's. There'd been weeks of dust and noise and roped off areas of the store. At least it wasn't busy season now, but still, the commotion every day was hard to take.

But Olivia was happy. Deliriously happy. There was that.

The bright spot in these past few weeks had been Barry joining her for evening drinks out on the point, watching the sunset. He'd come over a couple times a week after he'd stopped by to walk her home when she closed up Parker's. Now they walked home together almost every night and she really enjoyed his company.

She looked up from behind the cash

register counter to see Barry standing there smiling at her. It startled her to see him there right when she'd been thinking of him. She quickly covered her surprise. "Well, hello there."

"Hi, Donna. I came by to get a malt. Emily said that the malt shop is being dismantled and moved the end of the week. Wanted to make sure I got one last one in before waiting for it to reappear next door."

"Yes, they are tearing down the wall behind the malt counter and connecting it to the cafe next door."

"Do you have time to join me? You know it will be your last chance for a while." His eyes enticed her with the thought of a brief break.

"Let me get Lydia to watch the checkout. I'll meet you over at the malt shop."

She wasn't really hungry, but spending a bit of time with Barry was always a welcome break. She found Lydia, then went to join Barry and gave Olivia a break while she chatted with him.

She made their malts and settled onto a stool next to him. As usual, he talked about the Cabot remodel. Things were getting closer to being wrapped up.

"Donna."

She turned at the sound of her name, surprised to see Evelyn standing there.

"Evelyn, what's up? Have you met Barry? He's working on Cabot Hotel."

"No, I haven't. Nice to meet you."

"Barry, this is my sister, Evelyn."

"Great to meet you, Evelyn. Will you join us?"

Evelyn looked undecided.

"Come on, Evie, join us." Donna stood and went behind the counter.

"Maybe a scoop of vanilla. In a dish."

Donna got the ice cream and handed it to Evelyn. "So what brings you to Parker's?"

"My cell phone charger isn't working and I thought I'd pick up another one."

Donna frowned. "Let me think where we moved the display. I think it's over by the extension cords and lightbulbs. Used to be right up front, but everything is a bit... ah... disorganized right now with the expansion."

"I'll find it." Evelyn took a bite of her ice cream.

"So, Barry was just telling me about the work on the hotel. It's almost finished," Donna said to Evelyn.

"We're going to have a grand opening,"

Barry added. "A bit behind on planning it. I need to find someone to head that up. Usually, these kinds of events are planned much further in advance, but we weren't certain on how long some of the updates would take, and now Delbert doesn't want to delay the opening. We've done some preliminary publicity for it, but it's only six weeks away."

"I could help with that," Evelyn offered.

Donna had to keep her mouth from literally hanging open. "You'd help?"

Evelyn nodded.

"We'd pay you, of course," Barry added. "I have no idea what the going rate is for an event organizer, but at this point, I'd pay you anything you ask."

"Well, Evelyn is a whiz at planning parties and fundraisers. She'd do great planning your grand opening." Donna bragged on her sister, though she still was surprised she'd offered.

"I could come by and see the hotel, see whatever you do have planned, and take it from there."

"That would be great," Barry's face flooded with relief. "Really great."

"Do you have many ideas about what you

want?" Evelyn took a small notebook out of her purse.

Barry smiled sheepishly. "No... and I should have. Delbert wants a grand party. Open house style, but sending out invitations to local leaders, the mayor, chamber of commerce, some other people from surrounding areas. Really, whoever you think would come." He laughed.

"Evelyn knows everyone. She's great with exactly this kind of event. Well, not a hotel opening, but a big bash."

Evelyn blushed. "Stop it, Donna. Though, I do have a bit of experience with parties."

"You've thrown more parties and fundraisers than anyone I know."

"I'm grateful you'll take this on. Can you come by tomorrow morning and we'll hammer out more details?" Barry laughed. "Or should I say I'll let you hammer out more details. And I'll get the budget from Delbert."

"That works out fine. Say about ten tomorrow morning?" Evelyn took one more bite of her ice cream and slipped off the stool. "I'm going to go find the phone charger. I'll see you tomorrow."

Donna was still a bit stunned as her sister walked away.

Her sister was planning this party. Like a real job. Getting paid for it. She shook her head. Something was going on with her. She just knew it. Her sister hadn't held a job in her whole life. Never earned a penny. She'd gone directly from being daughter to wife without a single working life in between. And Darren had never wanted her to work. He wanted her there taking care of his every need. Planning his parties. Looking beautiful on his arm.

Barry handed her his empty malt glass. "That was great as usual. And it looks like your family is always providing just the person I need for my work."

"I'm sure Evelyn will do a brilliant job for you."

"Before I leave, I wanted to ask you something."

He stood across the counter from her, looking a bit... was it nervous?

"I... I wanted to ask if you'd go on another date with me. I need to go into Sarasota for this Chamber of Commerce joint meeting. It's people from the surrounding towns like Belle Island, Sanibel, Ft. Myers, Anna Maria Island. Kind of a mingle thing. Delbert offered up The Hamilton in Sarasota for the get-together. He thinks it would be a good idea to go and just get out the word about The Cabot Hotel reopening. I thought you might like to go... you could spread the word about Parker's expansion, too."

Her thoughts immediately went to wondering what to wear, then hopscotched over to realizing he was asking her on another date, then on to thinking that it wasn't a bad idea to talk up Parker's expansion.

He just stood there and she realized she hadn't answered him. "Oh, when is it?"

He laughed. "Bet that's a bit of crucial information. It's next Saturday."

"Yes, I could go. It probably is a good idea to get the word out about Parker's expansion." She blushed slightly at her awkward acceptance. "I mean, I'd like to go, thank you."

"It's going to be a fancy thing. Like suit and tie."

She sighed in relief thinking of that pretty black dress Olivia and Heather insisted she get. That would be just perfect to wear.

"I better run. I'll see you soon." He turned and left the store, leaving her with a girlish excitement she hadn't felt in a long time.

Olivia came up to the counter. "Mom, you okay? You look a little flushed."

"What? No, I'm fine. Just a bit hot in here today." She wasn't ready to tell Olivia about her date. And she might even get dressed for this one all on her own. She smiled as she walked away to relieve Lydia at the cash register.

CHAPTER 16

Barry pulled into Donna's driveway on Saturday evening. It seemed strange to even have the car out. He walked everywhere in Moonbeam these days and really enjoyed it.

He climbed out and walked up to her door, feeling a bit uncomfortable in his shirt and tie. He'd gotten used to the more casual attire here in Moonbeam. His suit coat was in the back seat of the car, ready to slip on when they got to The Hamilton.

Donna answered the door and he took in a quick gulp of air. She was stunning in a simple black dress, a silver necklace, and her hair pulled back in some kind of simple silver clip with loose tendrils framing her face.

"You look beautiful," he said admiringly.

Her cheeks flushed pink. "Thank you."

He couldn't take his eyes off her. Stunning, that was the only word that kept running through his mind. "Um... are you ready?"

"I am." She picked up a black evening bag from a small table by the door and came outside.

He walked her to the car and opened the door for her, admiring her long, tanned legs swinging inside before he closed the door.

They drove away from the house and silence settled over them. Donna turned to look at him, and he smiled.

"I'm a bit nervous about tonight," she admitted.

"Nervous? Why?"

"I'm not used to these fancy things. This is more in line with an event Evelyn would go to."

"Well, they aren't my favorite thing either, but I do go to a lot of them for business reasons."

"I don't know what to say to these people."

"Just talk to them like normal people. That's what they all are. Most will be small business owners or managers from the surrounding area. You'll do fine." Of course, she would. She was friendly and used to talking to people all day long at Parker's.

When they got to The Hamilton, he went around to open the door and help her out of the car. He reached into the backseat, grabbed his suit coat, and slipped it on. She took his arm —he liked the feel of her hand resting on his arm—and they walked in through the front door.

He'd never been to the Sarasota Hamilton before and the lobby was extraordinary. It was decorated in an understated elegance in light, welcoming colors.

"Oh, this is beautiful," Donna exclaimed as she slowly turned around, taking in the whole thing.

"Delbert does a great job when he buys up these old hotels and remodels them," he said as he too slowly turned to see the whole lobby, appreciating the architecture, the interior design, and the ambience.

He led her through the lobby to the large room where the event was being held. He snagged glasses of Champagne and waved to Delbert across the room.

"I should let you go mingle and talk to

people." Donna stood by his side looking uncomfortable.

He smiled. "Come on, let me introduce you to the few people I know here."

He made introductions, and as he expected, Donna was soon chatting away with an owner of a boutique on Belle Island and manager of a bridal shop in Ft. Myers. Then a constant stream of other people.

She finally turned to him at a break in meeting new people and laughed. "Okay, this is better than I thought."

He winked. "Told you."

Delbert made his way over to them. "You two having a good time?"

"We are," Barry said as he scanned the room. "Camille here?" She always seemed to be at Del's side at events like this.

"She... ah... couldn't make it."

"That's too bad." Though it really wasn't. He was still a bit ticked at her for hurting Emily's feelings. Okay, quite a bit ticked.

"This hotel is beautiful." Donna motioned to the wide wall of windows. "And so bright and airy in this room."

"Thanks. I'm hoping The Cabot turns out just as nice." Delbert laughed. "No, that's not right. I'm hoping it turns out better. I really do have a special place in my heart for that hotel."

"You do? Why?" Donna asked.

"When I was younger, I came to The Cabot for several summers for vacations with my grandparents. I have such fond memories of it. And I want to make sure she's restored to how grand she used to be."

"I think she will be," Barry said. "And the ballroom is turning out even better than I'd hoped. The old chandeliers are rewired and repaired. And Emily found old photos of the room and we've matched the room as closely as we could to how it was before."

"And I do like that there is still the polished reception desk all along the one wall at the side of the lobby. I'm glad you were able to use it. It looks so much the same. It just has computers on it now." Delbert grinned and turned to Donna. "And your Emily is quite the find for us. She's doing a great job with setting up the history alcove in the library. It's almost finished."

"She's really enjoyed working on it. I'm grateful you gave her the opportunity. I know she's quite young."

"And quite smart and has a world of

knowledge about the town." Delbert waved to someone across the room and turned back to them. "I guess I should go and mingle a bit. I see the mayor of Moonbeam. Must say hi and keep on her good side."

"Everyone is on our mayor's good side," Donna laughed. "I don't think she has a bad side."

Delbert walked off, shaking hands with people as he headed over to the mayor.

Donna turned to him. "So, Camille. She's the one who was so... ah... not nice to Emily?"

"She told you, huh?"

"She told Olivia, who told me. And she was in Parker's the other day. She was... let's just say not the friendliest person to Olivia."

"I'm sorry." He frowned. He couldn't imagine someone not being nice to Olivia. Or Emily for that matter. Camille was a difficult person...

"It's not your fault. It's just an... interesting pairing, Delbert and Camille."

A thought he'd had before himself. "Yes... it's..." He shrugged, not wanting to spend any more time talking about Camille or talking badly about his boss's choice in girlfriends. "Shall we go mingle some more?"

"Good plan." She smiled at him.

Donna was sure she'd met two hundred people, or possibly five hundred or a *bazillion*, here at the event. At first, she tried to remember all the names, but soon she realized that was impossible... She'd had a good time but now she was exhausted.

She'd tried appetizers that she had no idea what they were and switched to sparkling water after her one champagne. Her new black shoes were pretty, but her feet hurt after all the standing. She'd love to be home in jeans and bare feet about now. She was weary of the drone of conversations and struggling to remember faces and names. Too bad Evelyn wasn't here. She would have handled all of this with grace and charm. And probably had everyone's name straight, too.

It hadn't been as bad as she thought it would be, and she'd even really enjoyed it for a bit. But... she was over it now. She glanced around for Barry and suddenly he was at her side, whispering in her ear. "You ready to go? I'm kind of over the noise and people."

"I'm so ready." She nodded.

As Barry led her back out into the lobby, the din of conversation faded. Her muscles relaxed and tensions swept away every step they took. The cool air rushed over her as they stepped outside, and she took in a deep, cleansing breath.

Barry shrugged off his suit coat, loosened his tie, and unbuttoned the top button on his shirt. Then he grinned as he rolled up his sleeves. "I'm ready to get back to the more casual life in Moonbeam."

"And the quiet," she said as she got into his car.

They drove back to Moonbeam chatting about people they'd met and trying to decipher a few of the choices of appetizers. The motion of the car began to lull her to sleep, but she struggled to stay awake to keep Barry company on the drive.

Barry glanced over at Donna and smiled. She was sound asleep in her seat, her face relaxed and peaceful. He knew she'd do fine at the get-together, and she had. But events like that were tiring. He'd done his part, chatting about the opening of the hotel until he just couldn't bear it another moment. The crowded room, the buzz of conversation. He was glad Donna seemed ready to go when he was.

It was strangely intimate to be driving home in the darkness with Donna sleeping beside him. Okay, in her own seat, but still it was peaceful and calming after the hubbub of the evening.

He finally pulled into her driveway, leaving the car running, unwilling to disturb her. But he couldn't sit out here all night with the car running. She stirred a bit and he reluctantly shut off the car.

She blinked a few times, stirred again, then looked over at him with sleepy eyes and a sheepish look. "I'm sorry. I didn't mean to fall asleep."

"No problem. It was a long night."

She stretched her arms out and cocked her head from one side to the other. "It was, but now more people know about Parker's expansion and the opening of The Cabot, so we did what we'd planned to do."

"That they do." He got out and went around to open the car door for her.

She slipped out and walked to the door. "I'm

glad you asked me to go. I had a better time than I thought I would."

"I'm glad you did." He stood staring at her in the muted light filtering out the windows. More tendrils of her hair had worked loose and framed her face. She held her shoes in her hand. He understood that. He couldn't wait to get back to his house and kick off his dress shoes. Yet... he didn't want to leave her. Not yet.

Besides, maybe he should kiss her. *It sounded like a good idea, didn't it?*

She stifled a yawn and his manners kicked in.

"I better go. It's late." The kiss would have to wait. Besides, he wasn't certain it was a good idea or not.

She nodded. "Thanks, again."

He turned and headed back to the car and drove the one house over and pulled into the garage. Grabbing his coat and tie from the backseat, he headed inside. The house was deadly quiet and empty after the noise of the evening and the comfortable, intimate atmosphere of driving home in the darkness with Donna.

He slipped off his shoes and padded to the front window and stood staring at Donna's house. As he watched, the house darkened when she turned off the front lights. She was probably headed for bed.

Which he should do, too. But as tired as he was, he was wired, too. He headed through the house and out onto the small, screened lanai and sank into one of the comfortable overstuffed chairs. The sky was filled with twinkling stars and the moon cast a shaft of light across the water in the canal. The tide was coming in and the water lazily drifted past the dock in front of the house and onward. The tide changes fascinated him. He'd been surprised to see how far the water in the canals rose and fell with the tides.

He'd toyed with buying some fishing gear so he could fish off the dock, not that he had much free time. He sat outside, listening to the lullaby of the night sounds until sleep threatened to overcome him. He shoved out of the chair and went inside, reluctantly leaving the night behind him.

CHAPTER 17

Barry sat at the bar at Jimmy's out on the wharf, sipping a beer. It had been a long day at the hotel and he wanted to unwind before heading home. He turned when someone sat on the barstool next to him, then grinned.

"Well, hello there, Delbert. Looks like you had the same idea that I did."

"Looks like it." Del nodded to the bartender. "I'll have that local craft beer." He pointed to a sign up high above the bar. "It's been a long day."

Barry laughed. "I was just thinking the same thing."

"So, did Donna enjoy the get-together at The Hamilton? We sure had a good turnout."

"She did. And there were a ton of people there."

"By the end of the night, I'm pretty sure everyone knew about the grand reopening of The Cabot." Delbert smiled. "I even heard Donna talking about it to a group of ladies she was chatting with."

"I knew she'd have a good time. She's so easy to talk to, and people just seem to like her." *He* liked her...

"Oh, and I finally met Evelyn in person this week. Looks like she's doing a great job with the grand opening. She said she's calling it a gala. A 1920s theme. She has some great ideas and seems very capable."

"I think so, too. Glad to have someone else in charge of that. She's got catering set up and servers. Invitations went out weeks ago, plus basically the whole town of Moonbeam is invited."

"Sounds like it will be perfect. And I'll be glad when we get our official occupancy permits. Should be soon. I'm going to move into one of the suites for the last few weeks until we open." The bartender brought Del's beer and he took a sip.

"You are? Well, that's probably more convenient than staying on Belle Island."

Delbert stared at his beer glass for a moment, then looked directly at him. "I haven't been staying on the island. I've been driving into Sarasota and staying at The Hamilton."

"Really?"

Delbert let out a long breath and grimaced. "Seems that Camille and I are on the outs. I tried really hard with her. I did. She was charming and fun to be with when she wanted to be." He shrugged. "But she was a bit... difficult. And sometimes she could be a bit... um... self-centered."

And by self-centered, if Delbert meant mean girl, he'd agree with him.

"Anyway, I can't have her talking to my employees like she did to Emily, and it wasn't the first time. I'm always running interference between her remarks and people I care about. This deal with Emily was the last straw. She said she was heading back to Belle Island and..."

Barry stayed silent letting Del continue or not.

"She expected me to apologize for asking her to not interfere in my business decisions of who I hire. And I asked her to not speak to them like she did. I feel like people who work for me are my family. Camille? Well, she doesn't understand that. She was raised... differently."

"So, are you just taking a small break? Giving her time?"

"No, I'm thinking it's a permanent break. Honestly, I'm fond of her, but the woman wears me out with her demands and her acidic remarks to people. And... she tends to be a bit, ah, overly dramatic at times."

No kidding. And Delbert was one of the most down to earth people Barry had ever met. Even though he was in charge of all the new properties that Hamilton Hotels opened and was next in line to take over the whole company from his father. He did treat his employees well and people loved to get jobs at his hotels as evidenced by the massive number of applicants for jobs at The Cabot.

"I'm sorry it didn't work out for you two." Though, he really wasn't. He wasn't much impressed by Camille's whole attitude and couldn't forget the tears he'd seen in Emily's eyes when Camille made her dismissive remarks to her.

"It's for the best. Things have been rough for a while now. I just didn't have the energy to actually go through with explaining to her why things weren't working out. Didn't want to hurt her feelings. And—" Delbert grinned. "I'm sure it's better that *she* decided we should break up than I did. But it's just... well, breakups are tough, aren't they?"

He nodded. "They are."

"Anyway, as soon as the permits go through, I'll move in. It will be easier than commuting to Sarasota."

"Should only be a few more days."

"So, I'm starving, you want to grab a sandwich here or something?" Del asked.

"That sounds like a plan. I was trying to think what I had in the fridge to cook at home, and the pickings were pretty sparse. I'm not much of a cook these days. Just don't have the time." Barry figured Del could use the company tonight. He seemed a bit down—though possibly relieved—about the whole Camille thing.

"Perfect. Let's get dinner."

They had their meal, chatting about the rehab, and what was left to do on the finishing touches. An hour later they left, with Delbert heading to Sarasota.

Barry headed back to Sandpiper Court, by

now knowing his way all around town with no missteps in the wrong direction. He loved being able to walk everywhere. He'd miss that when this job was over. He doubted he'd ever get a job in a small town like this again. More's the pity.

His footsteps fell softly on the sidewalks as he walked home in the moonlight, feeling at peace and at one with his world, perhaps for the first time in his life.

CHAPTER 18

Olivia had been working from early mornings until hours after Parker's closed for weeks and weeks now, trying to get everything sorted out with the expansion. Things were going well, except when they weren't. They'd run into some glitches that cost more than she'd budgeted, but a few—very few—things came in under budget and she'd made a few cost-saving decisions.

The original section of Parker's was taking shape, at least. New lighting to brighten up the once dark corners. She'd scored on some old sturdy wooden shelving units from a store that was closing a few towns over. They made the perfect backdrop for when people entered the store, filled with items that were most needed by their customers.

The back section of the new building was connected first, floor refinished, and she'd moved so much of the lesser bought inventory over there so the original building wasn't so crowded. While she'd done that, they'd refinished the wooden floors in the original building.

She had to admit, she was pretty proud of how it had all turned out so far. All she needed was to get the as-yet unnamed cafe opened and the ice cream counter up and running again.

She looked up as Heather ducked under the rope blocking off the unopened section. "Hey, cuz."

"Hey, yourself. You've been scarce." Olivia put down the cloth she was using to clean the windows.

"You're one to talk. You've turned down my last two invites to dinner and you don't meet me at Brewster's for coffee anymore in the mornings."

"I know. I'm sorry. I've just been so busy."

She heard the front door to the cafe open and turned around to tell yet another person they weren't opened yet. Could people not read the sign on the door? The townspeople were curious, and many had stopped by to see how things were going. As she turned, she was surprised to see Aunt Evelyn standing there. She glanced at Heather and saw that her cousin was more surprised than she was.

"Hi." Aunt Evelyn walked further in, closing the door behind her. "I wanted to come see how things were coming along."

"Well, Parker's is doing great. You should peek in there. And we've expanded in the back of the building here. I just need to get the cafe up and running."

"How's that coming along?"

"It's... slow. I've got the permits for the kitchen, and this week the order of tables and chairs will be here. But I haven't found someone to do the baking to stock the bakery counter. I want to start with just baked goods, some really great coffee, and then we'll still have the ice cream counter, of course."

"I could," Aunt Evelyn said.

"You could what?" Heather asked the same question Olivia had been thinking.

"I could bake for the cafe. I certainly know Grandmother's recipes."

"But..." Heather's face held a puzzled expression.

"I think I might like it. I do love to bake." Evelyn glanced around the cafe but avoided looking directly at Heather.

"I know you do, Aunt Evelyn. And you're a wonderful baker. But this would be a full-time job and—" She wasn't certain if her aunt was joking... or what was actually going on here.

"Yes, I do believe I'll take this job." Evelyn nodded confidently.

"Are you sure?" Olivia hadn't known her aunt to ever work. Then again, she had taken the job planning the grand opening of The Cabot.

"I'm sure. The gala event for The Cabot is next week. After that, I'll be free and clear. How long until the cafe is ready to be opened?"

"I was hoping by the end of the month."

"Perfect timing, then. I'll finish up the gala, and in the meantime I'll drop by tomorrow. We'll start a list of ingredients to order. I'll bring my ideas on what items we could serve. I'm thinking we'll vary them each day?"

"Yes, whatever you think." Relief rushed through Olivia, but there was still the tiniest bit of apprehension that Aunt Evelyn would change her mind.

"Okay, then. See you tomorrow." Aunt Evelyn turned and left.

Heather sank onto a large crate. "I don't understand. Mother has never worked. Ever. And she took that job planning the gala for The Cabot, but I thought that was just this one-time deal because it sounded like fun to her. But now... she wants a full-time job?"

"Who wants a full-time job?" Donna entered the cafe.

"Aunt Evelyn just said she was going to take on being the baker for the cafe for Livy."

"No. She didn't say that." Her mother frowned.

"Yes, she did. Insisted she wanted the job." Heather got up and paced the floor. "I don't understand it. She just... doesn't work."

"Something is going on with her. I just know it. She's acting... different." Her mother's brow creased. "I think I'm going to head over to her house in a bit and talk to her."

"Good luck with that. Mother is never very... forthcoming." Heather picked up her purse. "I'm going to head out. I hope this works out for you with Mother taking the job. I just don't want you to get hurt or get left stranded."

"I'm sure it will be fine." But Olivia knew that was a lie. She wasn't certain at all.

~

Donna headed out a few hours later, determined to talk to Evelyn. As she walked out of Parker's she spotted Jackie and Jillian approaching. Unfortunately, they saw her and waved before she had a chance to duck back inside the store.

"Oh, Donna. There you are." Jackie hurried up to her with Jillian just steps behind. Both sisters' faces were flushed and Jackie was out of breath.

Although most people said they had a hard time telling the twins apart, she never had any trouble. Well, no trouble with telling them apart, just trouble with... them. And their gossip.

"So, how is the expansion going?" Jillian asked. "We tried to get into the new side, but Olivia chased us out. Said it wasn't safe to have people in there yet with all the work going on."

Olivia probably had just wanted to find a reason to shoo them out the door... Donna pasted on a smile. "Things are going great. Just great. Should be ready to open soon."

"Really? That's quick. I sure hope this whole expanding Parker's works for you. I mean, it's not like you were that busy anyway, were you?" Jackie shook her head.

"Business has been good. Great, actually." She didn't know why she was defending her store to these two, but if they were going to spread gossip, it might as well be gossip that Parker's was doing fabulously. Even if they were just doing... *okay*. And she hoped this expansion *didn't* tax their finances too much. But the Jenkins twins didn't need to know that.

"So..." Jackie leaned forward and lowered her voice in a conspiratorial whisper. "I heard that Evelyn has been talking to Steve Anderson, the new realtor in town."

"I wonder what she was talking to him about." Jillian added, her over-dyed locks of midnight black hair bobbing along with her head. "Do you think that she and Darren are looking to move? Though I can't imagine ever wanting to leave their gorgeous house. Right there on the harbor. It's lovely. And I'm not sure there's a larger, nicer house in Moonbeam to buy."

"She's probably just checking out the market value. She likes to keep up on those types of things," Donna said quickly. There was no need for the Jenkins sisters to know that Evelyn never cared about those kinds of things. At all. She let Darren deal with all things financial.

Jillian looked disappointed. "Oh, I guess that's probably right."

"Well, I've got to run." Donna glanced down the sidewalk, planning her escape. "Sorry I don't have longer to stay and chat."

She turned and hurried away before they could ask her anything else. But now she had questions of her own. Why had her sister taken a full-time job, and why had she been talking to Steve Anderson? And why would she talk to a brand new realtor instead of one who had been here for years in Moonbeam?

So many questions, and she was going to get some answers. She walked over to Evelyn's and rang the doorbell. The thought flitted through her mind that it was strange that she rang the doorbell at Evelyn's but her sister just walked into her house calling out she was there. Well, all the family just walked in and called out as they entered her home, and Evelyn was no exception.

She waited for a minute, then rang the doorbell again. Where was Evelyn's housekeeper? Even if Evelyn was gone, the housekeeper would answer the door.

Finally, the door swung open and Evelyn stood in the doorway, an apron wrapped around her slender waist, a surprised look on her face. "Donna, what are you doing here?"

Donna stepped inside without waiting to be invited. "I came to talk." She looked at the foyer and the long hallway off to the side. Boxes were stacked everywhere. She turned to Evelyn. "You want to tell me what's going on?"

"I'm just getting rid of a few things. Come, have some tea."

She followed her sister to the kitchen a frown resting on her face. Evelyn was not telling her something. She knew it.

Evelyn poured them some tall glasses of iced tea and led the way out onto her beautiful patio overlooking the harbor. They sat down in matching chairs.

Donna took a sip of her tea, set it down, and turned to her sister. "Okay, now talk to me. The girls told me you're taking a full-time job at the cafe. And you took the job with The Cabot coordinating their gala. I want to know why."

"Because—" Evelyn stared out at the water for a few moments. "Well, I enjoyed the work on the gala. And found I liked getting paid for the work. I love to bake. Why not bake for the cafe and help out?"

"Nice try. What are you not telling me?" She pinned her sister with a look that she hoped showed she wasn't leaving until she had an answer. A real answer.

"I don't know what you mean." Evelyn's face held a carefully crafted innocent expression.

"Evie, come on. Talk to me." She was certain her sister was not telling her everything.

Slowly Evelyn set down her glass, and Donna swore there were tears forming in her sister's eyes. She hadn't seen her sister cry in years. Probably since they were young girls. Her sister just... didn't cry. Not at happy events, not at funerals, not at sad movies. Never.

"I— I'm in a bit of a mess right now," Evelyn finally said.

She reached out and took her sister's hand. "What kind of a mess?"

"I have no money. None."

"What do you mean you have no money?" She frowned. This was the last thing she thought she'd hear from her sister. She and Darren had tons of money. Didn't they?

"It seems like Darren—" Evelyn closed her eyes for a moment, then they fluttered open again. "Darren left me."

"He what?"

"He left me. And when we got married I signed all these papers. Didn't really know what they said, but I trusted Darren. It seems though, in the event of a divorce, I'm left with... nothing. Only what I earned during the marriage. And you know that Darren never wanted me to work..."

"That can't be right." Donna squeezed her hand. "We'll talk to a lawyer."

"I have, actually. Two of them. Both of them said the paper was ironclad and that I should never have signed without having a lawyer look at it. But, of course, I did. I was young and foolish." Evelyn stood and walked to the edge of the patio. "So, I'm boxing up some things that were gifts and a dealer is coming to get them. I'm hoping to get some money from them. I've been boxing up my personal items. I have thirty days to move out of the house."

"No." She jumped up and went to her sister's side.

"Yes. I mean, I can't afford the house, obviously."

"This isn't right."

"But it is what's happening. He's moving back in with... someone new."

"Oh, Evie. I'm sorry." She'd never liked Darren. At all. But even this was low for him.

"After all those years and everything I did for him... I was such a fool." Evelyn took a deep breath, her eyes filled with regret. "Anyway, I need a place to live and a job. I need to learn to support myself."

"You can move in with me," Donna offered.

"Oh, I couldn't impose on you like that."

"You're not imposing. You're my sister. Of course, you'll move in."

"You sure you don't mind? It will just be until I can find a place I can afford."

"For as long as you need."

"Thanks, Donna." Evelyn sighed. Her usually composed sister looked almost... defeated. "There's so much to deal with. I've packed up my personal things. I've already sold some of the jewelry Darren gave me. I don't really have anything to call my own in this house. My kitchen things that I bought are about all I'm taking. I've sent a lot of my fancy clothes to the resale shop. I won't be needing those for fancy country club events anymore. I was wondering why they didn't ask me to help at the last fundraiser at the club. I guess the men at the club knew about this and told their wives..."

"Evelyn, I'm so, so sorry." She hugged her sister even though her sister wasn't a hugging person. She figured Evelyn could use the hug whether she knew she needed it or not.

Evelyn actually returned the embrace and clung to her for a moment, then she pulled away, straightened up. "Let's go sit back down and finish our tea."

"So, what can I do to help?" Donna asked as they settled back in their chairs.

"Giving me a place to live for a bit will help. It helps a lot."

"If you need money—"

"No, I'm fine for now. I'll sell some of my things. I still have some jewelry to sell. At least Darren showered me with expensive jewelry and original artwork. I want none of it now. None. So it makes it easy to sell off."

"Oh, Evie." Her heart was breaking for her sister. For Darren's betrayal. For her financial situation. She wondered how her sister would weather all this. Evelyn had always had it easy her whole life. She'd been taken care of. Given every luxury.

And now... she had nothing.

No, that wasn't right. Evelyn had her family. And Donna was determined they'd all help her through this.

CHAPTER 19

The next evening after work, Donna started cleaning out a closet in a guest room for Evelyn. She also needed to clear out the garage. Somehow, over the years with just her one car—not that she drove it often—half the garage had managed to fill up with boxes. She needed space for Evelyn, her car, and her things, and wanted her sister to feel welcome.

She got out bags to donate some of the clothing in the closet, unsure why she had kept some of the outfits. Probably because it had been easier to move them into an extra closet than deal with getting rid of them. Well, the thrift shop in town was going to get a haul soon.

She cleaned and dusted the room, putting

fresh linens on the bed. She wasn't sure exactly when Evelyn would move in, but she wanted the room ready and waiting for her.

"Mom, you here?" Olivia's voice drifted up from downstairs.

"Up here."

Olivia clattered up the stairs and poked her head in the room. "What are you doing? Weird time of day for a cleaning spree."

"I'm—" She paused. It wasn't her place to tell Olivia what was going on in Evelyn's life. But she'd know sooner or later when she saw Evelyn moved in. "I'm cleaning the guest room."

"Obviously. You getting ready to have company?"

"No. I mean, yes." She sighed.

"Mom, what aren't you telling me?" Olivia stood in the doorway, her hands on her hips.

Might as well tell her now. The truth would be out soon. "Evelyn is moving in with me."

"She's what? Why? That doesn't make any sense. Is her house getting treated for bugs or something?" Olivia's forehead creased as she tried to sort out what she'd heard.

"No, she's moving in here to live. At least for a while."

"She have a fight with Darren?"

"No... not a fight." Donna sank onto the bed. "Darren is divorcing her."

"He isn't." Olivia shook his head. "I never saw that coming. I didn't think he'd give up the woman who made his life easy, planned his parties, and charmed his business contacts."

"It appears he's found someone new."

"The jerk. Aunt Evelyn is way too good for him anyway. But why is she moving out of her house?"

"Ah... that. A bit of legal trouble. Well, a lot actually. She was so young when she married Darren. She signed papers he told her to sign. And now... she has hardly anything to her name, and it looks like Darren doesn't have to split anything with her."

"That's not right."

"I know. She helped him get where he is today. And he never wanted her to work. He wanted her there whenever he wanted her to do anything."

"She needs to talk to a lawyer." Olivia sank onto the bed next to her.

"She has. Two, she said. It doesn't look hopeful."

"So that's why she took the job as the baker at the cafe. She needs money."

"And why she took the job planning the gala."

"Poor Aunt Evelyn." Olivia shook her head then paused. "Does Heather know?"

"I'm not sure. She hasn't said anything to you?"

"Not a word. And I'm sure she would."

"It's not our place to tell Heather. That's up to Evelyn."

"That's going to be almost impossible. Heather always knows if I'm hiding something."

"You'll have to be careful, then. It's not ours to tell."

Olivia sighed. "I know, but still, it will be hard. She's going to be so mad. She's going to be furious with her dad."

"I'm sure she will be. They don't get along very well in the best of times."

"That's because he's a big jerk."

"Olivia, don't call your uncle names." But Olivia was right. Darren *was* a jerk.

"Heather is going to explode when she finds out."

"Maybe. But you need to let her work things

out with her father. She still has the right to have some kind of relationship with her dad, even if her parents divorce."

"I know you always encouraged me to have a relationship with Dad, but that never really worked out, did it?"

"I never stood between you and him."

Olivia frowned. "No, you didn't. He just wasn't very interested in having a relationship with me."

"And I'm sorry for that. He missed a lot with you." Donna couldn't understand why her ex-husband, Charlie, made so little effort to see Olivia or Emily. But that was his choice, not her interference.

"Well, I'm going to head home. And try to avoid Heather until she comes to me and rants about what Uncle Darren is doing to Aunt Evelyn."

"Okay, good night, sweetie."

Olivia got off the bed to leave.

"Oh, why did you stop in?" Donna asked.

"Right, that." Olivia laughed. "Wanted to borrow your blender. Ours broke and Emily is on a smoothie kick. I ordered another one but it won't come for a few days."

"Sure, just grab it on your way out."

"Thanks, Mom. See you tomorrow."

Donna turned back to the project at hand, boxing up clothes to give away and clearing out the dresser. It was going to take longer than she thought to conquer this room.

CHAPTER 20

The next evening Donna closed up Parker's, touched the sign by the door, and turned to make her way home.

"Hey, Donna. Wait up." Barry came jogging up to her. "I was hoping I'd get here before you closed up so we could walk home together."

"Looks like you're just in time." She smiled, glad to have the company. She'd been worrying about Evelyn all day, and problem after problem kept cropping up at the store. She couldn't wait to get home and kick off her shoes.

They headed out toward Sandpiper Court, walking side by side.

"You look tired," Barry said, then laughed. "I guess that's not really something you want to hear, is it?"

"I am tired. Long day."

"Want to unwind with a drink when we get home?"

"That sounds lovely. Can you give me about fifteen minutes to change clothes and meet me out on the point? Just come around back in the pool cage."

"Sounds perfect. Don't mind if I slip on shorts and a t-shirt myself. It's warmed up a bit since I first got here. The nights aren't chilly anymore."

They got to their houses and Donna changed into casual clothes, opened a bottle of red wine, and reached for the glasses.

She heard a knock at the slider between the pool cage and the kitchen and motioned for Barry to come in.

"Red wine okay? Or there's beer in the fridge."

"Red wine is perfect." He nodded toward the doorway to the garage. "What's with all the boxes?"

"Ah, that." She sighed. "Let's go outside and I'll explain."

They went out to the point and settled into the chairs. She poured the wine and took a sip. A hint of a light breeze ruffled the palm fronds and stars glistened in the sky. A perfect coastal night.

The solar twinkle lights in the mason jars cast a mellow yellow light on the small table. A round ceramic ball with cutout star shapes glowed at the very end of the point. Whoever came up with solar lighting was a genius as far as she was concerned.

She leaned back in her chair and relaxed, then turned toward Barry. "So Evelyn is going to move in here with me for a while."

"Really?" He raised an eyebrow.

"She needs a place to stay for a time."

"I thought she was married and had a big house on the harbor." He grinned sheepishly. "Emily was chatting with me about her."

"She was... is... married. Though, she soon won't be. Her husband is divorcing her."

"Oh, I'm sorry."

"I'm not. He's... well, he's not a very nice man. Super controlling of her. And a snake. He had her sign a paper before she married him, and let's just say she didn't know what she was signing and now she's walking away from a long marriage with almost nothing."

"That doesn't seem right." He frowned.

"It's not, but evidently the papers are legal. She was young and didn't know better."

"I'm sorry for her troubles."

"That's why she took the job planning the gala for the hotel. And after that gala next week, she's going to start working at the cafe when it opens. She's a talented baker and... well, I hope it works out for everyone. Olivia needs a baker. Evelyn needs a job."

"She's never let it show that she's going through all that. She's worked long hours pulling off the gala for the opening. She never even looks stressed with juggling all the details."

"That's Evelyn. She's rarely ruffled over anything. Can juggle a million things at once. But this... it's hit her hard and I want to do anything I can to help her."

"If I can do anything—anything at all— you'll ask me, right?"

"I doubt if there's much any of us can do. I already offered to help her financially, but she said no. She wants to do this on her own. At least she accepted my offer to live here while she sorts things out."

"You're a good sister." He smiled.

"Anyone would do that for family." She shrugged off the compliment.

"Maybe. Maybe, not."

The more Barry learned about Donna, the more he was...

He was what?

Attracted to her? He admitted that. He considered her his friend now after all the time he'd been in Moonbeam and all the time they'd spent together. It was comfortable being with her. Fun. Familiar.

And yet there was something between them. An undercurrent. A pull. He was certain.

Well, fairly certain.

"So, I heard from Emily that you got the final go-ahead permit-wise on opening The Cabot."

Her remark pulled him from his thoughts. "We did. Delbert has moved in through the opening, helping with the last-minute things. And, of course, Evelyn has everything almost ready for the gala. I'm hoping everything goes smoothly."

"I'm sure it will."

They sipped their wine until he saw Donna smother a yawn. He took his last sip and stood. "I should go and let you get some sleep."

"I'll walk you out." She stood and grabbed the wine bottle and her glass.

He followed her into the kitchen and reached around her to set his glass on the counter. She stood just a foot from him and slowly turned, looking up at him.

He should back up. Give her some space. He should.

He stared at her, at her warm hazel eyes and the somewhat questioning look on her face. He took a quick breath and reached out a hand—

"Grams? You here?" The front door banged opened and he recognized Emily's voice.

He quickly took a step back and Donna sidestepped away from him.

"In the kitchen, Ems," Donna called out.

Emily rushed into the kitchen. "Sorry to bother you. Oh, hi, Barry."

"Hi." He nodded, still trying to collect himself after the tumultuous interruption.

"So, Mom borrowed the blender yesterday, but didn't bring the blade or that rubber gasket thingie for it and our new one still hasn't come. Miss my smoothies in the mornings."

"Oh, it's probably still in the drawer." Donna pointed.

"Great, thanks."

"I should go." He nodded at Donna. "I'll let you two find the parts and pieces you need."

"I'll walk you out." Donna led the way to the door.

He turned back as he slipped through the door. Donna gave him a questioning look and a weak smile. "Maybe I'll see you tomorrow night? Drinks again?"

"Yes, that sounds nice."

He turned and walked over to his rental. Just his luck to have Emily come crashing in right when he'd worked up the nerve to kiss Donna. He sighed, hoping that he'd soon have another chance. Like maybe when he saw her tomorrow night. Maybe they'd be alone...

CHAPTER 21

O livia did her best to avoid Heather.

That lasted two days.

Her cousin had called and begged her to meet at Brewster's this morning. She tried to beg off with the fact she was so busy at work, but Heather wasn't having it.

Maybe Heather knew about her mom and dad and that's why she wanted to meet her? But it was unlike Heather to not just blurt out what was happening.

She sighed as she reached the wharf and started walking down the pier to Brewster's. Halfway there, she spied Jackie and Jillian. She quickly glanced left and right, but there was no way to escape. They waved cheerfully and hurried up to her.

"Oh, Olivia. It's so good to see you," Jackie or Jillian said.

"Good to see you... but I'm kind of in a hurry. Meeting Heather."

"Oh, look, there she is. Right down the pier a ways." The other twin waved madly. "Yoo-hoo! Heather. Over here." This twin turned to the other one. "Look, now we have two Parker girls to talk too."

Not really a Parker... but that never stopped the town from calling them that.

Heather came walking up to them and looked about as excited as she had been to see the twins. "Hi."

Olivia sent her a quick not-my-fault look.

"Oh, Heather, dear. Jillian and I were so very sorry to hear about your parents." Okay, so that must be Jackie talking. But what did they know about her aunt and uncle?

"Right, thanks." Heather shrugged.

"These things happen, I guess. But we *are* sorry." Jillian said, nodding so vigorously that she looked like a bobblehead. "And someone else? That's just shameful."

"Right." Heather still looked noncommittal.

Olivia gulped and grabbed Heather's arm.

"Well, we have to run. I don't have much time until I need to get to work."

"Tell your mother if there is anything we can do, to just ask us," Jackie said. "Of course we'd do anything to help her, poor dear."

Olivia dragged Heather toward Brewster's. When they got further away from the twins, Heather stopped and turned to her. "What in the world were they talking about?"

A sinking feeling hit the pit of her stomach. So Aunt Evelyn hadn't talked to Heather yet. "Um... I'm not sure."

Heather stared at her. Stared at her hard. "Yes, you do. I can tell."

"Heather—I—" She swallowed. "Let get our coffee and sit."

"And you'll tell me?" Heather pinned her with a no-nonsense look.

"I'll tell you. But it's not really mine to tell."

"But you'll tell me because you're not only my cousin, you're my best friend and we have no secrets."

Well, they'd had a secret for two days. It appeared like the secret was out. Or would be in another moment or two. Olivia wished she'd just told Heather she couldn't come this morning. It would be easier than... this.

They got their coffee and a table away from any other customers. Olivia blew on her cup of coffee, trying to find the right words, annoyed that Aunt Evelyn hadn't told Heather yet.

"Livy, talk."

"It would be better if you went and talked to your mother."

"And I will. But first, you'll tell me what you know."

"I can't. I don't know how to tell you this." Olivia set down the cup.

"Just tell me." Heather's face was a stony mask of dread.

"Okay." She took a deep breath. "Your dad asked your mom for a divorce."

Heather's eyes flew open wide. "He did?"

"Yes."

Heather frowned. "But why wouldn't Mom tell me?"

"I don't know. But obviously the word is out now since the Jenkins twins know. And who knows how they found out. Of course, they seem to find out everything that happens here in Moonbeam. And if the twins know it, soon the whole town will be talking about it."

"But why would he divorce her? She does everything for him. I doubt if he even knows where the dry cleaner is to take his clothes to. And who will plan his business functions? And... well, Mom is beautiful. I always thought he liked being married to someone so glamorous and capable. She made his personal life and business life so easy for him. Not to mention he's a hard man to please. I don't understand..."

"I don't know the details. But listen, I'm pretty sure there are financial issues, too."

"Father lost his money?" Heather's forehead creased.

"Um... no... more like your mother lost any money."

"Surely there's a settlement. Mom should get half of what they have, right? They've been married forever."

"There's some kind of legal paper she signed before they were married. I don't think she's getting much of anything."

Heather's eyes flashed. "That is so like him. Always in it for himself. Expecting perfection from everyone, but so underhanded himself."

"Anyway, she's going to move in with Mom for a bit until she sorts things out. It appears your dad is taking the house and um... moving someone new in with him."

"That—lowlife, that scum, that scoundrel."

Olivia let out a small laugh. "I don't think I've ever heard someone actually use the word scoundrel."

"I have more words to call him... but... I won't. Oh, wait, scalawag."

"That's another good one."

Heather looked down at her coffee, then back up. "How's Mother doing?"

"I haven't seen her since I found out. But Mom says she's pretty rocky."

"I should go see her."

"Yes, you should."

"This is why she's been taking these jobs, isn't it?"

"Probably."

"I could help her out with money."

"Mom offered to help out financially, but Aunt Evelyn turned her down."

Heather stood. "I've got to go. I'm going to track down Mom."

She watched her cousin thread her way through the tables and disappear. She sat and finished her coffee, wondering how all this was going to work out. Aunt Evelyn living with Mom and working at the cafe. Would Heather stick around for a while now? And would Aunt Evelyn adjust to a working life?

So many questions. But one thing was certain. Uncle Darren *was* a scalawagish scoundrel. And if that wasn't a real term, it *should* be.

Heather rang the doorbell at her mother's house, but no one answered. She walked around back to see if her mother was out on the patio, but no sign of her. She peeked through the windows. Nothing. Too bad she didn't still have her key to the house. But then she knew her father had changed the locks to the house the day she'd told him she was moving out all those years ago... so there was that.

She remembered the days leading up to her escape in excruciating detail. He'd lit into her as soon as she came home one evening. Her scores on the entrance exam for college were not acceptable even though they were in the top three percent. He moved on to the fact that her outfit was unacceptable—simple shorts that weren't even that short and a t-shirt from Lighthouse Point. She and her friends had been at the beach and she thought her clothes were perfectly fine for that.

Her mother had tried to change the subject and he told her to be quiet. He did that a lot. Dismissed anything her mother said.

He started listing off new rules for her. Curfew. What friends she could see. What colleges she would be applying to. What classes she'd be taking. And then said he'd have to approve any outfit she wore out of the house.

She'd gone upstairs without even arguing back. That should have given him a clue. She'd stayed for exactly one more month. Luckily she'd saved up money from various jobs and stashed it in an account he didn't know she had. She squirreled away some of her personal things she wanted like her art supplies and books and some of those exact same clothes he disapproved of. Olivia had taken boxes of things for her.

Then one night she'd come home, and her father started yelling at her when he found out she'd dropped out of the debate club. She'd had to so she could work more hours after school to earn money, but he didn't know that.

Her mother tried to change the subject once again, and he turned and screamed at her, her mother's face draining of all color. That's when she knew she had to move out.

She was just causing more trouble for her mother. She'd gone upstairs, packed a duffle of belongings, and traipsed back downstairs and into the living room where her father was reading and her mother was writing on some endless list.

She told them she was leaving and her mother begged her to stay. But her father? He'd said goodbye and he was tired of dealing with such an ungrateful and totally unacceptable child. She still remembered the words... *totally unacceptable*.

She'd moved in with Aunt Donna and Olivia for the rest of her senior year of high school, then moved from Moonbeam the day after she and Olivia graduated.

"Heather?" The French door opened, and her mother's voice drew her away from the haunting memories.

"Mom. There you are."

"I just got home and saw your car in the driveway."

She threw her arms around her mother and hugged her tight. She couldn't remember the last time they'd had a real hug. She clung to her for a moment, then stepped back. "You should have told me."

"So you heard. Come in." Her mother closed the door behind them.

"The Jenkins twins know."

Her mother let out a long sigh. "Well then. Everyone one will very soon, won't they?"

"They will. But we don't care."

"I guess I should try to track down my own mother and tell her before she finds out from someone else. Though, I think she's still off on her world travels."

"So, it can probably wait until she's back home, right?"

"You're right. I don't think I'm ready to hear her opinion on this. I'm fairly certain she'll think it's all my fault."

"Probably." Her grandmother totally approved of her mother's marriage. Thought that Darren Carlson was the ultimate marriage material. But then, he'd been so like her grandfather. Domineering and demanding. Maybe grandmother just thought that was how powerful men were and everyone had to take it.

"There's nothing I can do about that. I'll tell her soon."

"So, what's this I hear about Father taking everything? Leaving you with nothing? We'll fight it."

"I've already talked to two different lawyers."

"We'll find another one."

"Well, in the meantime I need to move out and learn to support myself."

"I can help money-wise. I can loan you money. *Give* you money. Anything. This art thing of mine... ." She shrugged, unsure of what to say. "It's kind of worked out for me and I... I kind of invested in Livy's cafe and the expansion at Parker's."

"You did?" Her mother cocked her head. "I didn't know. Why didn't anyone tell me?"

"Looks like our family is good at keeping secrets." She quirked an eyebrow up and grinned. "Aren't we?"

"Yes, I guess we are. And thanks for your offer of help, but no, it's time I learned to make it on my own. I don't want to be dependent on anyone ever again." A determined look was etched on her mother's face.

A strong look. Stronger than she'd ever seen before. Where was this look for all those years when her father had harangued her mother endlessly? Well, she was glad to see the look there now. Her mother would need to be strong to get through this.

"You could live with me if you want."

"Oh, Heather, I appreciate the offer, but your condo is small and it only has the one bedroom. I'll live with Donna until I can save up some money and find a place of my own. She has that whole big old house."

"Father's a snake." Heather's face flushed with the heat of anger, furious that he'd do this to her mother, his wife, after all these years.

"Well, be that what it is, I still need to move out."

"Then let me help you pack and I'll take a load of things over to Aunt Donna's for you."

Her mother looked at her gratefully. "I'll accept that help. Between trying to pack up what I need and finishing up the last-minute details for the gala, I admit to being overwhelmed."

"I'm here to help. Anything you need." And at this very strange time in life, she felt closer to her mother than she had in years.

CHAPTER 22

Donna looked up and down the street after she touched the plaque by the front door of Parker's and locked up the store. But there was no sign of Barry in either direction. She'd thought that maybe he'd stop by and walk home with her. Vague disappointment seeped through her, but that was silly. She was perfectly capable of walking home alone. And she had a lot to do. She'd cleaned out the room for Evelyn but hadn't finished dealing with all the boxes lined up in her laundry room and spilling into the kitchen.

She glanced at her phone when it pinged with a text from Heather. She and Evelyn were on their way over with a load of Evelyn's belongings. Good thing she got the room cleared out.

She hurried home, dropped her purse on the table by the door, and kicked off her shoes. She wondered if they were going to stay long because Barry had mentioned coming over tonight for a drink...

She padded barefoot into the kitchen, thinking about making a quick sandwich for her dinner.

"Aunt Donna?" Heather's voice rang out as she entered the house.

So much for that sandwich. She turned to go help them. Heather and Evelyn stood inside the doorway with their arms laden with boxes. "Just take them up to the guest room. The one you stayed in when we were girls. I'll go out to your car and grab some things and help bring them in."

The three of them made numerous trips outside and then upstairs until both Evelyn and Heather's cars were empty. Afterward, Donna poured them all glasses of tea. Heather sank onto a stool by the island in the kitchen. "I'm beat. We must have packed a million boxes today."

"Heather helped me take some boxes to

storage, too," Evelyn said as she slipped onto the stool next to Heather. "She's been a big help."

And look at that. Heather and Evelyn getting along. This was an improvement. "Good. I'm glad you had help. When do you plan to move in here?"

"A few more days. After the gala, if that's okay."

"Anytime is fine with me." Donna leaned against the counter, tired from the long day at work and the multiple trips up and down the stairs with Evelyn's things. She heard a knock at the door and glanced at her watch. It was probably Barry. She'd have to send him away. Evelyn needed her now.

"Want me to get that?" Heather started to climb off her stool.

"No, I've got it." Evelyn went to answer the front door. Barry stood there with a bottle of red wine and a warm smile.

"Oh, Barry. I'm sorry. I'm going to have to cancel."

She couldn't miss the disappointed look that flashed through his eyes, though he quickly covered it with another smile.

"No problem. Maybe later this week."

"Maybe. I mean, sure. It's just... Evelyn is moving in, and well, things are complicated."

Barry looked uncertain and shifted from foot to foot. "Okay, then maybe you could just let me know when you have some time?"

"Yes, I will. It's just right now is... tough."

"I don't want to bother you."

"It's not a bother. I want to spend some time with you, it's just—" She looked past Barry and frowned as a car she didn't recognize pulled into the drive. The door swung open, and Donna leaned against the doorframe in surprise.

Well, this would be interesting.

Her mother stepped gracefully out of the car, dressed precisely in country club casual complete with high heels. She glided toward them—because gliding was how her mother always walked. There was really no other way to describe it.

Barry stepped back as she approached, looking at her mother then back at her, a questioning look in his eyes.

"Donna, what are you doing standing in the doorway letting out all the air-conditioning?" The ever-familiar critical frown was etched on her mother's face.

"Mother. Welcome home."

Her mother stared pointedly at Barry.

"Mother, this is Barry. He's working on the renovations of The Cabot and he's renting the house next door. Barry, this is my mother, Patricia."

Her mother looked from Barry's face down to the bottle of red wine in his hand.

"Pleased to meet you." Barry gave her mother a smile.

"Yes. Same," her mother answered.

What kind of greeting was that?

"I should go." Barry took another step back and she nodded.

"Thanks. Sorry about tonight." She shrugged and gave him a weak smile. They needed to talk, but the time wasn't right. She thought life had gotten complicated with Evelyn moving in. Now she could add her mother back in the country to the list of complications.

Barry nodded once and turned to head back home as her mother breezed past her and into the house.

Sure, go right in, Mother.

Evelyn and Heather stood in the entranceway from the kitchen.

"Mother," Evelyn said and walked close to

give her a quick, perfunctory peck on the cheek. "You're home."

"I am. Didn't you pay attention to my itinerary?"

Evelyn looked guilty. "I guess I just lost track of time."

Donna had lost track of time, too. *And* lost the itinerary. "Well, we're glad to see you," she assured her mother.

"Hi, Grandmother," Heather added.

"You're all here. Isn't that a nice surprise?" But somehow her mother's voice didn't sound pleased as she floated past them all and into the kitchen. They followed in her wake.

"Here, Mom, would you like some tea?" Donna reached for the pitcher.

"No, thank you. I don't do caffeine this late in the evening."

"Water?"

"No, I'm fine." Her mother looked around and her gaze settled on the stools and drinks at the island. "Are you all just *perching* here in the kitchen?"

"Ah... we were just going to sit down at the kitchen table." Heather grabbed her glass and headed to the table. Donna sent her a grateful glance.

Her mother slid effortlessly into a chair and they all took seats around her. Her mother glanced over at the stack of boxes leaning like a falling tower in the corner.

"What are all those boxes?"

"I... uh... I was just clearing out some things. Going to send some things to the thrift store," Donna quickly said, glancing over at Evelyn, not sure if her sister was ready to tell their mother the news about Darren.

"I see. Well, they really clutter up your kitchen." She smoothed an imaginary wrinkle from her pristinely pressed slacks with her tanned hands that sported an impeccable manicure.

Evelyn's eyes filled with apprehension. Donna sent her a look of encouragement. Even though Evelyn had always been her parents' favorite—that had always been evident to everyone—her mother was not going to welcome Evelyn's news.

"Mother..." Evelyn started, paused, took a breath, then continued. "I'm moving in here with Donna."

"Why in the world? Oh, are you redecorating your house? I know it does need a slight refresh. Houses get like that. Good for you for jumping on it before it gets out of hand."

Donna couldn't think of even one thing that needed updating at Evelyn's house...

"No, it's not that. It's..." Evelyn looked over, her eyes pleading for help.

"She going to live here for a while." She came to her sister's aid.

Heather jumped to her feet and went to stand behind Evelyn. "Father's leaving Mom. He's asked for a divorce."

"No, that's ridiculous. He wouldn't do that." Her mother frowned. "There would be talk and it might hurt his business."

"He did ask me for a divorce. Well, not in person. He sent papers by courier. That's how I found out."

Donna's eyes widened. That's one detail she hadn't known.

"You should try and work things out with him. Get him back." Her mother frowned. "That's the right thing to do." Her mother looked at Evelyn critically. "Maybe you could update your haircut. You need a new dye job, too. We could go shopping for some new clothes..."

"Not happening, Grandmother." Heather put her hands on her mother's shoulders.

"But she should. That's what we do. He's her husband." Her mother honestly looked confused.

"Not for much longer, Mother. He doesn't want to work things out. He's found someone new."

"He'll tire of her. They always do and come back."

Donna looked at her mother with new eyes. Had that happened in her parents' marriage?

"Mother... I don't want him back." Evelyn simply shrugged. "Ever."

"That's just foolishness on your part." She stood and took her expensive clutch off the table. "Pure foolishness. You need to rethink that stance. He'll come back."

"Mother——" Evelyn started to speak.

Her mother held up a hand. "No more foolish talk. Try to work it out." With that, she swept out of the kitchen, the door closing firmly as she left.

"Welcome, home, Mother," Evelyn said softly.

CHAPTER 23

The next evening Donna sat with Heather, Olivia, and Evelyn in her kitchen. They'd all had long days. Evelyn had put the finishing touches on the gala. Olivia had solved about a million problems that had come up with the renovation of Parker's, and Donna was beginning to question whether they'd made the right decision. Heather had helped her mother with the gala and gone over and hauled more of Evelyn's things to storage.

"Hey, where is everyone?" They turned at the sound of Emily calling out.

"We're out here, Em," Olivia called through the open door to the main room.

Emily rushed out, her arms full of garment bags. "Guess what."

Donna smiled at her granddaughter's enthusiasm. "What?"

"I found out about this costume shop and I rented costumes for the gala. It's set in the nineteen twenties... so I got all of us clothes to wear. Just look." She opened up bag after bag of elegant twenties-style ballroom gowns. From full-length to flapper length complete with gloves and hats.

"Oh, Emily, those are such fun." Evelyn stood and admired the outfits.

"I guessed the sizes and got a few extras. The lady at the shop said she'd been having a run on twenties' outfits the last week. I think a lot of people are dressing the part for the gala."

"Well, that will settle the question of what I was going to wear." Donna admired a long silvery gown that looked just her size.

Emily laughed and handed it to her. "I knew you'd love that one." She turned to Evelyn and handed her a sapphire full-length gown that had a classic cut to it. "And I thought you'd like this."

"It's perfect." Evelyn reached for the gown.

"Mom and Heather, I got you some flapper dresses. And I got this one for me."

Donna gaped at the lovely formal gown that

Emily held up. It was an emerald green shimmering fabric, ankle length with a dropped waist. It would set off her granddaughter's pretty green eyes so nicely.

"It reminds me of a dress in one of those old Cabot portraits I found." Emily held the dress up and admired it.

"These are all perfect, honey." Olivia hugged her daughter.

"I'm so excited. I've never been to an event like this. I can't wait for people to see the history alcove, too. The whole hotel looks magical. You should see what Evelyn's done with the ballroom. It's so enchanting... just like you stepped back in time."

"I can't wait to see it," Donna was excited to see what Evelyn had done to the ballroom.

"I can't wait either." Emily danced around the kitchen, holding her dress up against her. "It's going to be a magical night."

Donna stood in the doorway, waving goodbye to all of them. They were all coming back to her house tomorrow to get ready before the gala, then they'd go early to help Evelyn with anything she might need. They would all drive together since parking space would be limited. The gala promised to be every bit as magical as Emily insisted it was going to be.

She glanced up at the starry sky and then over to Barry's house. Faded light drifted out from his windows. Maybe she should call him. Invite him over. But then, it was really last minute and she still felt guilty about sending him away last night.

And right that minute, Barry stepped out onto his front porch. He glanced over and saw her standing there in the open doorway. Her mother's voice ricocheted through her mind. *And letting out all the air-conditioning.* She smiled in spite of herself.

Barry waved and she waved back. He pulled the door closed behind him and walked over to her front porch. "Hey."

"Hi." Suddenly she was shy with him. Uneasy. Uncertain. "Um... do you want to come in and have a drink?"

"Yes. I mean, no. I mean—" He raked his hands through his hair, standing there in the moonlight looking impossibly handsome.

She stood there, uncertain whether he was coming in or not.

He took a step closer and touched her arm. Electricity boomeranged through her, and she looked down where his hand rested on her arm, almost surprised to not see a burn mark there from the heat between them.

He reached his other hand out and tilted her chin up to look at him. "Let me start again. I've been wanting to talk to you. There's something between us, isn't there? I mean, I feel it. You do too, don't you?" He looked directly into her eyes.

Her heart fluttered and her pulse swept through her like a raging tide. She stared at his face for a moment before answering him honestly. "I do."

"Great. I feel better knowing I'm not imagining it." Barry grinned, relief evident on his face.

"No, it's there. Something is definitely there." She'd felt it for weeks now. Maybe longer. But had been so unsure if she'd imagined it. Guess not.

He gently pushed a lock of hair away from her face. "I want to kiss you."

"You were going to kiss me the other night when Emily interrupted us, weren't you?"

"I was." He gave her a smile that sent her pulse racing and jumbled her thoughts.

She could barely breathe but managed to get a few words out of her tangled thoughts. "You probably should." She couldn't take her eyes off his, locked together, frozen in the moment.

The world seemed to stop as he leaned down and kissed her. Her stomach fluttered, and her hand, with a mind of its own, crept up around his neck, pulling him closer.

He pulled back finally and sighed. "That was... nice. Excellent even." His bemused smile charmed her even more.

"It was," she agreed.

It *was* a perfect kiss. One full of the promise of new beginnings. A chance to figure out just exactly what *was* going on between them. She wasn't certain what it was, but there was *something* there. Something special.

She smiled up at him, looking deep into those captivating sky-blue eyes of his. She didn't need a gala to have a magical night. Tonight was one.

And he kissed her again in the moonlight while the world continued around her in slow motion and she savored every moment.

CHAPTER 24

Donna loved what she saw in the mirror. The silvery gown floated over her figure, hiding her imperfections and somehow making her look... well, better than she'd imagined was possible. She fingered the silky, smooth fabric with pleasure. The gown was perfect.

She turned to watch as all the Parker women finished getting ready for the gala, crowded into her bedroom. Her room filled with laughter and happy chatter as they all got dressed. Family time at its best. She could feel the love and strength of these women surrounding her.

Olivia walked up behind her in a flashy flapper dress, the fringe on it swishing back and forth at her knees. "Mom, you look great."

"So do you." She turned. "All of you do."

"This is going to be so much fun." Emily moved in front of the full-length mirror, turning this way and that, admiring her emerald green dress and looking incredibly older than her sixteen years.

"You look lovely, Em." She kissed her granddaughter's cheek, her heart swelling with love for the girl. For all the Parker women.

"Thanks, Grams."

"So, is everyone ready to go?" She glanced over at her sister, looking stunning in the sapphire gown Emily had picked out for her. And, for now, the sad look that had settled on Evelyn's face was gone and her eyes were shining in anticipation.

"I can't wait. Tonight is going to be wonderful." Heather walked up and put her arm around her mother. "Everyone is going to see what a great job you did planning this party, Mom."

"I hope it all goes off without any problems." Evelyn adjusted the long strand of pearls draped around her neck.

"Knowing you, you have every single detail under control." Heather laughed.

Donna took one last look in the mirror.

"Mom, why do you have that look on your

face?" Olivia whispered to her as everyone finished getting ready.

"I'm just excited about this evening." She wasn't ready to tell anyone yet about why she was so... happy. Her world felt different today after Barry's kiss last night. Things had shifted subtly. She was excited about the gala. Excited about seeing Barry there at The Cabot. She could still feel his kiss on her lips. But she sure wasn't going to share that fact with her daughter.

Okay, just one more peek in the mirror. Really, *one* last look. She turned around slowly in front of the full-length mirror. Yes, the dress was perfect. It was going to be a fabulous night, surrounded by family... and Barry.

"Okay, let's go." She grabbed her keys and drove everyone to The Cabot. A large banner stretched across the grounds proclaiming the gala and the grand opening. She parked the car and they all got out and stood for a moment, enchanted by the lighted circle drive leading up to the hotel, the doors wide-open like a siren call to come inside.

"This is so exciting." Emily danced around, swishing her dress.

She slowly turned her gaze to look at all of

them, these Parker women. They looked like they'd all stepped right out of the nineteen-twenties.

Even with their challenges with the expansion of Parker's and Evelyn's impending divorce hovering around them, it still felt like life was pretty darn perfect.

"Are we ready?" Donna stepped onto the festive circle drive and linked arms with her sister, then Olivia and Heather joined them, and finally Emily—after stopping her excited twirling—linked arms with them, too.

And all the Parker women walked into the gala, arm in arm, for what she was sure would be a magical night, just like Emily predicted.

Dear Reader,

I hope you enjoyed this first book in the Moonbeam Bay series. Ready for more stories? Try **The Parker Cafe**, book two in the series!

Book two is Livy's story. And, of course, you'll read more about Donna and Barry. And how is Evelyn doing with all the changes in her life? Hope you enjoy it!

Do you want to be the first to know about exclusive promotions, news, giveaways, and new releases? Sign up for my VIP Newsletter on my website.

kaycorrell.com

Or join my reader group on Facebook. They're always helping name my characters, see my covers first, and we just generally have a good time.

facebook.com/groups/KayCorrell/

As always, thanks for reading my stories. I truly appreciate all my readers.

Happy reading,

Kay

COMFORT CROSSING ~ THE SERIES

The Shop on Main - Book One

The Memory Box - Book Two

The Christmas Cottage - A Holiday Novella
(Book 2.5)

The Letter - Book Three

The Christmas Scarf - A Holiday Novella (Book 3.5)

The Magnolia Cafe - Book Four

The Unexpected Wedding - Book Five

The Wedding in the Grove (crossover short story
between series - Josephine and Paul from The
Letter.)

LIGHTHOUSE POINT ~ THE SERIES

Wish Upon a Shell - Book One

Wedding on the Beach - Book Two

Love at the Lighthouse - Book Three

Cottage near the Point - Book Four

Return to the Island - Book Five

Bungalow by the Bay - Book Six

CHARMING INN ~ Return to Lighthouse Point

One Simple Wish - Book One

Two of a Kind - Book Two

Three Little Things - Book Three

Four Short Weeks - Book Four

Five Years or So - Book Five

Six Hours Away - Book Six

Charming Christmas - Book Seven

SWEET RIVER ~ THE SERIES

A Dream to Believe in - Book One

A Memory to Cherish - Book Two

A Song to Remember - Book Three

A Time to Forgive - Book Four

A Summer of Secrets - Book Five

A Moment in the Moonlight - Book Six

MOONBEAM BAY ~ THE SERIES (2021)

The Parker Women - Book One (Jan 2021)

The Parker Cafe - Book Two (Feb 2021)

A Heather Parker Original - Book Three

The Parker Family Secret - Book Four

Grace Parker's Peach Pie - Book Five

INDIGO BAY ~ Save by getting Kay's complete collection of stories previously published separately in the multi-author Indigo Bay series. The three stories are all interconnected.

Sweet Days by the Bay

Or buy them separately:

Sweet Sunrise - Book Three

Sweet Holiday Memories - A short holiday story

Sweet Starlight - Book Nine

ABOUT THE AUTHOR

Kay writes sweet, heartwarming stories that are a cross between women's fiction and contemporary romance. She is known for her charming small towns, quirky townsfolk, and enduring strong friendships between the women in her books.

Kay lives in the Midwest of the U.S. and can often be found out and about with her camera, taking a myriad of photographs which she likes to incorporate into her book covers. When not lost in her writing or photography, she can be found spending time with her ever-supportive husband, knitting, or playing with her puppies —two cavaliers and one naughty but adorable Australian shepherd. Kay and her husband also love to travel. When it comes to vacation time, she is torn between a nice trip to the beach or the mountains—but the mountains only get considered in the summer—she swears she's allergic to snow.

Learn more about Kay and her books at
kaycorrell.com

While you're there, sign up for her newsletter to
hear about new releases, sales, and giveaways.

WHERE TO FIND ME:
kaycorrell.com
authorcontact@kaycorrell.com

Join my Facebook Reader Group. We have lots
of fun and you'll hear about sales and new
releases first!
https://www.facebook.com/groups/KayCorrell/

I love to hear from my readers. Feel free to
contact me at authorcontact@kaycorrell.com

facebook.com/KayCorrellAuthor

instagram.com/kaycorrell

pinterest.com/kaycorrellauthor

amazon.com/author/kaycorrell

bookbub.com/authors/kay-correll

Made in the USA
Middletown, DE
19 May 2024